Tezcatlipoca's Dream

Una novela corta (en inglés)

HENRY GREEN

DEDICACIÓN

Para Princess

And about those other cacti, further away, like an army advancing uphill under machine-gun fire. All at once there was nothing to see outside but a ruined church full of pumpkins, caves for doors, windows bearded with grass. The exterior was blackened as by fire and it had an air of being damned.

Malcolm Lowry – Under the Volcano

CONTENIDO

PREFACIO

Boom! The sixteen canons on land signaled farewell to all those at sea, but it was also a rally call for people to come and say goodbye to the ships headed back to Spain.

Boom! The gun decks at sea acknowledged the signal and marked the start of their long journey across the waves to show off wealth and curiosities plundered from this corner of the New World; New Spain. As the gun smoke cleared, it revealed an angry sky. The golden hour in the Tropics was usually serene but today it looked as though the gods had other plans.

On the deck of *The Pangaea*, the crew was a flurry of activity.

'Bo'sun, go below decks and secure anything that's even remotely loose. We're going to pitch and roll with the devil before this night's through.'

'Couldn't we wait, Captain? Until tomorrow perhaps?' Started Bo'sun Rodriguez.

'Damn it, man! I shall not have my orders questioned. That last shipment of treasure from Guanajuato has delayed us enough already. The Crown needn't know that your incompetence has made us two days late. Now jump to it, and ask your second mate to calm the horses as best he can, before I change my mind and whip you for insubordination. Lord knows you deserve it!'

Rodriguez ducked below decks letting his eyes quickly adjust to the gloom and his nose to the smell which was not yet wretched so early in the voyage but bordered on putrid nonetheless. Three decks down where the horses were stabled was darker still and the fetid air made him gag as he looked for the second mate. The Bo'sun took a deep breath of fresh air at a nearby porthole and started to check on the horses. The one nearest him, black and bold looked familiar and despite kicking nervously let himself be touched on the muzzle. A faceful of hot horse breath was the last thing Bo'sun Rodriguez wanted but he took it in his stride and wished he'd had something to give him in return like a carrot or maybe an apple. Perhaps the impending departure was making his taste buds remember simple food pleasures from home. The scent of the soldiers' and sailors' sweat mingling with the horses'.

'Don't worry boy, there's a storm coming and I'm going to tie your ropes tighter if that's ok with you?' He fastened the ropes to the iron rings in the floor and wall and repeated the same action for all fifteen mounts. 'God has seen fit to throw us some bad weather, boy, but we will pray and we will survive, so don't you worry.' Next he quietly sang a song he thought might be appropriate for horses;

> May your head be strong
> May your heart be true
> May your legs be swift and your tail bright
> On your back, Pegasus, you'll carry us all
> As if the burden's light...

and he threw more straw into each of the troughs.

The captain's mere mention of Guanajuato gave Bo'sun Silviano Rodriguez reason to reminisce, sure enough. They had been stationed there – they had helped to build and craft and plan that jewel of a town – for nearly two years. He missed it with his whole heart.

Quanax Ranax, the biggest prize of all, standing proud and white amidst its green rolling hills. But it was a woman who had stolen his soul. Isabelle, a local beauty who was betrothed to one Jose-Ignacio, and soon to be the mother of his only child. Despite Silviano's strongest protestations he had been persuaded, by those that knew of his predicament, to accompany the treasure fleet and flee before Jose-Ignacio rearranged his features.

'You must leave,' even Isabelle had pleaded, 'don't you see that Jose-Ignacio will kill you outright?'

'Then I will stay and fight him.' Rodriguez had puffed up his chest.

'Your pride will be the death of you, and I don't have the stomach for such a duel. Please leave, so that I and the baby may live.'

He remembered that night because Isabelle had let him take her, by mule, to the hill above the new silver mine in the light of the full moon. They picnicked on chilaquiles that she had made and red wine that he had brought especially from the Spanish army's provisions. She had let him make love to her for the last time and both had cried as the mule brayed in defiance, its plaintive plea heard for miles in all directions. Bo'sun Rodriguez threw a stone at it and they both laughed.

'Please leave,' she said again more gently, before kissing him.

In his local pulquería Jose-Ignacio drew another pulque's froth through his moustache and begged forgiveness from their new patron saint the Holy Mother Mary Magdalene for the hundredth time that night. He was already heroically drunk, but numbed from grief it seemed there was no limit to the quantity of alcohol he could consume and he mumbled his catechisms into the tankard. He was a simple man with strong hands and a strong heart, full of courage and moral correctness, but not piety. Jose-Ignacio knew right from wrong and believed that what he did in life had consequences in the after-life. He did not want to go to hell, and prayed again to Mary before ordering yet another cup of the intoxicating maize beer. Mary Magdalene's statue stood behind the bar and watched him drink – he was convinced – feeling his pain. He didn't like the way she stared. Boom! The sound of the explosive charges was still ringing in his ears. Ever since the Spaniards had struck it rich in the silver mines all the local men and boys were busy round the clock extracting the precious metal with little or no regard for their welfare. His fingernails were broken and bleeding from digging through the rubble after it had collapsed on top of his father and four brothers, and pulling out their lifeless bodies. He would have his revenge and asked Mary to forgive him. If it meant going to hell, so be it, anything to wipe out this scourge of Spanish soldiers who enslaved and killed them, ravaged their women and stole their silver and gold. No, this Mary would not forgive him, there was another god he must curry favour with.

'Por favor?' He implored the bartender to lend him his ear.

Seconds later a silver coin was pressed into the barman's hand and Mary's likeness was replaced with a plain black cross.

Only Tezcatlipoca, the Prince of Darkness and Lord of the Smoking Mirror could help him now. After burying his family he would follow the soldiers to the sea and do what had to be done. He could hardly look his sweetheart, Isabelle – soon to be the mother of their first child – in the eye until he had squared justice. His chest swelled with pride at the thought of it and a smile formed at the corner of his thin-lipped mouth but it was short lived; she should not see him like this, full of pulque and bile, and bent on revenge. Tears rolled quietly down the strong man's cheeks.

The weeklong ride to the sea was anything but easy. The soldiers struggled with their heavy loads of treasure and munitions and Jose-Ignacio, hot on their heels, also had his fair share of problems as heavy rains made him cold and he did not have the luxury of being able to change animals. He had met with several other gangs of marauders and thieves along the way and wherever they could they had clashed with the Spaniards and drawn blood with their swords.

For the conquistadors, tropical storms had made rivers of previously dry canyons and mudslides had taken several of their pack mules as well as men who had lost their lives trying to protect the precious cargo against the elements. Ambushes had taken their toll. Bandits both white and black had done their best to chop off this money-serpent's head by force. It was well-known that there was a backlog of payments from the mining towns in the mountains to the Vatican in Rome. Swords had clashed and sparked, and more than once they'd left their wounded behind after battle, pushing on in order to meet the ships rather than rest and tend to casualties. Dead bodies were dumped in pools at the bottom of waterfalls, thrown off cliffs or hastily buried under piles of round stones.

But meet the ships – lying idly at anchor – they had, albeit forty-eight hours later than planned.

Jose-Ignacio arrived at the sea bloodied and exhausted. From the edge of the tree-line overlooking the ocean he watched his enemies preparing to embark on their long journey home and he cursed them. With arms outstretched against a sable sky he climbed to the highest rock and called upon Tezcatlipoca to bear witness.

'Lord of the Darkness, I implore you. Sir, I beseech you; avenge the death of my father and brothers – as I have done – with the blood of the Spaniards. Let all who plunder our nation's wealth, rape our women, and sully your great name O Lord; let all who set foot aboard these ships meet their untimely end at the bottom of the sea.'

There was no audible answer, yet from the dark clouds on the horizon the big man swore he saw lightning, and he felt satisfied.

For the sailors it would be a night to remember, and for many it was their last. The wild sea simply opened up and showed no mercy as it dragged their bones to the bottom. Of the eight ships, five were lost. The small remaining flotilla of three ships sighted the Spanish mainland at last light on Friday the 17th October 1515. On board ship there was much excitement that evening, and by daybreak the sailors were ready for home as they approached Europe and the Old World after an absence of two years.

'Our little town has changed it would seem,' the Captain remarked to Rodriguez.

'I think it is us who have changed, Captain. We have travelled to a new world and seen much that old Spain can only dream of. This old town sparkles like a new toy to me, but there is much that is familiar and comforting like returning to my mother's cooking.'

'Yes, Rodriguez. Ever the romantic sod. Before you taste your mother's cooking we must report to the Palace and pay these taxes to the Church.'

'I'll wager there are many fine hand maidens at the Palace only too pleased to welcome weary soldiers home!! Look, how even here they line the streets.'

'You'd best get to your station Bo'sun. I've a mind to keep you on board and stop you getting yourself into trouble. It's women that got you into this predicament in the first place, have you not forgotten? Now be off with you before I reach for my lash.'

Crowds of women and children lined the docks and ran alongside the slowly moving fleet. Hats and other bunting were tossed into the air. Tradesmen, horses and wagons to offload the treasure and goods from the fabled New Land waited in line. An armed escort of six equieries stood at attention awaiting Bo'sun Rodriguez and Captain Martinez.

To make landfall again after so many weeks at sea was no easy task. The sailors were weakened and weary after their ordeal, excited but tired. The monotonous diet of baked ship's biscuits and alcohol had left many men ill. Those already injured from fighting were in need of much more than bedrest. The air on board below decks had long ago turned fetid and the barrels of water that remained, were now fouled. Of the hundred or so soldiers who had survived all looked towards the heavens to thank God for delivering them safely and said a silent prayer for those that had perished. What those who had seen it were not saying was that they had found in Mexico City a metropole bigger and better than anything they had yet built in the Old World. The people were not savages and they had been welcomed warmly by their Emperor. This was not part of the plan and might not sit well with those who had funded the expedition and believed they were the mightiest and most righteous people on Earth. Captain Martinez knew he would do well to keep such thoughts to himself. He wondered, out loud, if the equieries could not first take him and the Bo'sun to bathe before being presented at court?

Indeed they could and the small band of weary travellers trotted briskly through the thronging crowds, to shouting and cheers of welcome and merriment. Martinez was pensive, knowing they had blood on their hands and was not one to champion the slaughter of their hosts. Spain, his homeland, sparkled less brilliantly than the hills of the jewel Guanajuato they had carved out of the Sierra Madre. He daredn't let the Bo'sun know how he felt, for fear that his sentimentality would be seen as treason. The sun caught the soldiers' polished helmets and the tips of their sharpened pikes, the triangular flags fluttering in the breeze as they rode through the city with all of its squalor and once familiar, now revolting, smells. As they turned away from the docks and began their journey towards the palace the streets became muddy with effluent and toothless whores grinned from wooden door frames. Beggars shuffled legless through the mire to request alms. They were nearing the baths and Martinez thought again of where they had been and what they had done there.

'Captain, anyone would think it was you who had left his fiancée behind. Why so gloom-ridden?' Asked Rodriguez.

'That is none of your concern.' Replied Martinez.

The palace kitchens were readying themselves for the celebration banquet and certain new foods had caught the attention of the below stairs team. 'Let me taste it, let me taste it!'

'Get your hands off, you moron. They'll kill you upstairs if you touch this before the King has had his fill.'

'Please Señora, por favor. Dame el chocolate saboroso.'

The staff had been busy ever since word had first reached them that sails had been sighted in the distance. Captain Martinez and Bo'sun Rodriguez had brought their flotilla back from the New World to an old order who eagerly anticipated them as returning heroes. Chillies, cocoa beans, potatoes, pimento beans, peppers now lay scattered about the kitchen surfaces bringing vivid colours and pungent aromas to the eyes and nostrils of the assembled cooks, housemaids, and butlers. Copper pots and pans were full to the brim with broiling chickens, pigs' heads, beef shins. Ovens were full of roasting beef, whole chickens, and quails.

'Pray Captain, which of these treasures would you consider your most valued possession?' The King had received his emissaries and was eagerly inspecting what had been brought up from the ships and displayed in all its glory in front of him.

'If I may?' It was Bo'sun Rodriguez who stepped forward. At that instant the Captain started to open his mouth but the King beckoned Silviano to speak.

'I believe there is something more beautiful and valuable than all this silver and gold.' His arm took in a vast array of treasures including multi-coloured parrots, jaguars on leashes, humingbirds in cages, capibarras, Indian slaves, as well as several open casks full to the brim with gold and silver.

The King's interest was piqued. 'Señor, I think you have our attention umm…'

'Bo'sun Rodriguez, your eminence.'

'Señor Rodriguez. Please show us which is your favourite.'

'If it pleases the court,' began Silviano, 'I would ask for complete darkness.'

'Enough! Bo'sun, I will lynch you if these games do not cease this instant.' Captain Martinez was red in the cheeks.

'Come captain, where's your sense of fun? I for one am intrigued. Besides there are hundreds of armed soldiers surrounding our treasure. Nothing can go wrong. You! More wine. You! Extinguish these lamps and you, Bo'sun! Continue. Por favor.'

With the palace in darkness, Silviano removed the silk cloth that covered his most prized possession – Tezcatlipoca's mask. He had never before set the mask on his face, yet his moves now were not his own, everything came to him instinctively.

The mask began to glow green and gold with

Silviano's eyes replaced by deep pits of red fire. The walls and ceiling of the palace, even the floor, disappeared and for a brief moment everyone was suspended in amongst the stars.

'Um a laa la oom. Um a laa la oom. Um a laa la oom.' The slaves began to chant as they recognized *their* king. One by one the wild animals also began to respond to this ancient call with a high-pitched wail that threatened to perforate the ear drums of all those in the room.

Silviano suddenly found himself in the high Andes. He had never been there and yet knew instantly that this was Tezcatlipoca's palace; the fabled Lost City. Through shifting mists he found himself looking down upon a city of opulence beyond his wildest dreams. Glimpses of lush terraces, bustling streets and plazas that dazzled with their brilliance. Just then he was wrenched back to the present and the palace. The Captain, not prone to flights of fancy, had managed to prise the mask from Silviano's face. It was not easy and he had burned both hands in the process, but his desire to throttle Rodriguez had overcome any irrational thoughts about ancient demons.

'Rodriguez, damn you! What are you doing? Are you trying to kill us? Take this man outside and execute him!'

'Esperense, wait!' it was the King, 'let him speak to us of this wonderful object.' His voice tinged with avarice.

Speech did not come straight away, however, and it was only after two goblets of wine that Silviano found his tongue.

'I bring this gift to you O King, as it once belonged to another more ancient king whom many still worship as a god. His name is Tezcatlipoca.' And with that he fainted.

After the reception at the palace there was indeed time for Bo'sun Rodriguez and Captain Martinez to go home and visit their families. It was a ride of some ten days, but a journey they intended to enjoy nonetheless.

The first day they took the road which climbed steeply out of port and arrived at the top of the handsome sea cliffs. With the Bo'sun's various and not insignificant appetites satiated he could look forward to the road and his eye took in the beauty of his homeland uninterrupted by any stirring in either his loins or his stomach. The cirrus clouds floated too high and too few to warrant rain; the city's terracotta rooftops fell beneath them and the mountains rose up in front of them beyond the pine forest through which they were yet to ride. They would aim to leave the trees behind them and overnight the other side of the ridge where they might find shelter from the seaward winds.

Silviano's lead horse was not one of his but a loaned animal from the Captain's cousin. He was a skewbald with something of an unruly temperament. The second saddle was a lovely bay mare but she looked almost too small to carry him on such a long journey. It irked someone as self-aware as Silviano that they should arrive home under such apparent ignominy but he would never let such emotions be known publicly, particularly not to the Captain.

They all did well through the cobbles of the town section and the slippery needles of the pine forest, but once they had reached altitude above the forest on the exposed slopes, the piebald began to complain vociferously. It quickly became cold and the sun was replaced by a crescent moon. Silviano looked back across his right shoulder and saw the ships in harbour like tiny specks below. From the treeline behind them came an unfamiliar low-pitched growling.

Silviano drew his sword and shouted, 'Who goes

there? Show yourself!'

A wolf stepped out of the gloom and began to bare its fangs. It hunched ready to pounce and eyed first the mare and then the man who danced towards him bravely with his flashing sword. The captain arrived seconds later as the wolf nimbly avoided the Bo'sun's blade and took a bite from Silviano's calf, tearing his tendon. The Bo'sun fell on his haunches and lumbered in pain to spin around as more wolves poured over the rocks ahead of them and their four horses. The wolf who had taken Silviano down moved in and took his victim's neck in a fatal stranglehold, while another alpha male faced the Captain and quickly bit his flailing sword arm. The wolfpack circled the kicking horses making good use of their speed and the horses' fear. With both men wounded or dead the piebald made a break for it before skidding and allowing two wolves to spring on top of him as he fell. Ironically, the small mare lasted longest, able to climb quickly onto the rocky slopes but her defiance was shortlived.

In the town below, few people slept well that night as the sound of the howling wolves seemed closer and more menacing than usual. Tezcatlipoca's breathing was hard and fast as he licked the blood from his pointed nose. He slunk away to stand on the rocks overlooking the moonlit sea and howled high and long, allowing the other wolves to eat their fill. The Lord of the Smoking Mirror smiled inwardly at the beauty of the seascape, but it was a shallow grin more satisfied with the killing.

PRÓLOGO

Tezcatlipoca had just made love to a nun and the irony was not lost on him. The chapel had been perfectly decorated with candles throughout, and the crucifix loomed large, both above the bed and around the nun's neck at the center of a long string of wooden beads. Her hair had been done up in a bun when he removed the habit's headdress and had then tumbled down her milky white shoulders as he drew her nearer, pulled out the bone hair pin and gently bit into her novice's nipples. For that's what they were, she can't have been older than fifteen.

He had taken the form of a French prince and chosen the brothel on the banks of the Seine as a retreat worthy enough of his somewhat eclectic needs. Whores, and many of them, opera and wine. At home he was losing a battle. The useless emperor Montezuma vexed him, his military losses were now spiritual losses for Tezcatlipoca whose enemies had gained ground in the netherworld.

As requested his nuns (there were enough for a nunnery) had left their lady-hair unshaved and he picked one of the nearest, lifted her scented petticoat and buried his head deep into that most holy of places, a sanctuary denied him when he took his throne as King of the underworld and Lord of the Smoking Mirror.

They needn't have asked if he wanted more wine and couldn't on account of their vows of silence, his goblet was kept full even as he drained it. Tonight it was only claret, another reason to choose France. He had no hankering for the crude alcohol of his patria. The nun on whom he had bestowed the favour of burying his beard between her legs was now offering an alternative that pleased him and meant that she would fellate him whilst there would be little or no wine drinking as she spread her legs and pushed her buttocks towards his face. Tezcatlipoca's long tongue devoured what was on offer and his loins thus stirred he called back the novice so that he could conquer her once more. She carefully sat across him while the other nun also sat up, still facing away from their lord and the two were inclined, not to kiss exactly, but to touch breasts as each took their own pleasure.

'Ladies, I am lost for words.' He said in his best French as they had all finished. 'You have humbled a royal Prince. I am now but a lowly pauper, a mere slave to your rare beauty and exceptional talents. Let it please you all to take what is owed from my purse. Now go. I will be gone by the time you are dressed.'

He took half from a round loaf of bread and pushed inside it two roasted quails. He took his horse and left the convent's gates behind him. He needed to think. Having eaten and drank more of the claret his mind's wheels began to turn with the oiling. Sooner or later the imbeciles were bound to discover his mountain lair and would plunder whatever riches they could get their hands on filling helmets and saddle bags with gold and silver. His enemies circled his corpse like vultures as if it were already dead. They wanted the mask and would do anything to get it. He in return would use his superior cunning in order to best hide it and outwit them.

INTRODUCCIÓN

In my mind's eye I am penning the great American (Mexican) novel from an upstairs window of a stone clad cottage overlooking the sea. Whitecaps catch the summer breeze and I sip iced tea and gaze at sea gulls suspended on the wind, giantlike, from my desk. In reality I am on a bus, scribbling in a notepad with Walkman headphones on. 'Are you a writer?' The woman next to me with two large brown bags of groceries asks.

'Well, not really.' I say and then wish I'd said something better, angry that I've lost my line of thought. Words are like songs, when they come complete with music and lyrics you have to stop everything and write them down or lose them forever.

'Don't let me stop you,' she continues. 'I can see you've got a good rhythm going.'

Recently my mom gave me a book I might ('would' or 'should') like. A highly acclaimed first novel by a young man about Mexico, Year of the Jaguar. It's the perfect gift for her son studying Mexican literature and about to go off in search of his biological father and literary heroes in the Mexican Sierra Madre. But I am oversensitive and such a 'normal' present makes me angry. It's not Mom's fault. The book is good, better than my rough draft by a mile and I burn everything I've written in a fit of pique. I look up from the paper and the shopping lady is still attentive, keen to continue asking questions. I fix my frown and bring my nice-eyes back into the game.

'Where are you headed? Airport?' It was the airport shuttle bus, but she raised an eyebrow towards my rucksack.

'Mexico. It's part of my studies.'

'Oh wow. My husband and I have a place in Baja. We go every year. I know it's not the same as real Mexico. Oh, I'm so jealous. You'll love it, dear.'

More than anything I wanted to be a writer. I made my way to the Hotel Oxford (the name and the price called to me). I flicked through the porn channels and was confronted by good retro-hardcore. Moustachioed men in dungarees with big dicks doing top-heavy blondes in bikinis. I would bus north to Guanajuato but not before I'd seen a bit of the capital.

In Mexico I felt free, not scared or awed. The thin air and the hazy sunlight filled me with excitement. I hit the streets and started to walk. Straight away the number of VW Beetle taxis caught my eye. Beggars in dirty bandages like soldiers in a forgotten war. Taco stands filling the air with the smell of hot oil and maize. Juice stalls making fresh papaya, strawberry, mango and melon smoothies. Tortas, tamales, quesadillas all fresh and delicious. Soft drinks, refrescos, sold in bags – like goldfish – with straws. Blaring music from boom boxes on every corner.

Every plate of greasy pig skin in chilli, every bowl of refried beans, every beer with lime as I sweated under the ceiling fan, I thought of my heroes – arriving by boat, arriving by road – as young men clutching D.H. Lawrence and Malcolm Lowry, ready to liberate (and poison) their minds with mescal and peyote to find the real Mexico and emulate Hart Crane.

I was drunk every night and threw up every morning for a whole year. Thirteen months, in fact. It was 1992 and I was twenty, turning twenty-one. This is the story of how people's lives can become so intertwined that boundaries are blurred until close friends, lovers, enemies even, become one another. As much as it is a story about Mexico, it is also a tale of love and death. It opens like all good Mexican stories, in a bar. Think loud and hot, but not so loud you can't hear the cicadas under a moonless sky filled with stars.

I was playing pool with my friend Buck in our favourite bar; a place called Rocinantes. One of the local gangsters – whom we knew by sight – asked me in Spanish if we wanted to bet on the game? I said did he mean for money?

'No,' he replied and pointed to Buck, saying 'his face.'

The bar felt sticky and loud. Another hot night. Open windows didn't do much to dissipate the clouds of smoke which hung in the air, nor did the slowly spinning ceiling fans. Rock and roll blasted through the speakers.

Buck perched on the edge of a table by the saloon doors which led out of the pool room's annexe and back into the bar's main drinking area. His teacher's briefcase was wedged securely between him and the wall, ready for a quick escape should he need one. He sucked on a Bohemia through his trademark moustache and stared into space. Luckily he hadn't heard above the music and general drunken chatter what had been discussed and already pissed that this guy had pointed at him was now impatient just to play pool.

He motioned to me, 'What's he saying, Henry?'

'They want to play for money.' I said into his ear. I had a lit Marlboro Light in one hand and a cold Dos Equus oscura on the go in the other.

The same gangster pushed through the small

crowd, stood up to Buck and said in English, 'We play for his face.'

Here I will interrupt because it's clear — well, it would be clear if you knew Buck at all — that this would soon blow up into a big, bloody battle with pool cues and bottles. Instead the fight which ensued had a very different outcome; it became an internal struggle that Buck had with himself not to tear this guy and all of his friends into a million pieces based entirely on his promise to me — made at my behest some minutes earlier round the corner — that there would be no fighting tonight.

We did play pool because it suited the gang who were hell-bent on taunting Buck, and we were good, winning fair and square. Plus I had my eye in, being on the table nearly every night and one of only two people in the world allowed to play with the owner's cue; the other person being the owner himself, Pompeiio. Buck was consistently the fall guy, the butt of all their jokes and he put in a superhuman effort to ignore them until one of their number moved an object ball after a foul shot — permissible under local rules — which they knew would annoy the shit out of him.

Buck grabbed the weaselly cholo by the throat intending to bite off his nose and brain him with the ball when Pompeiio burst through the saloon doors and told us to get out, that he'd give us a head-start on the gang. We had his word.

Outside in the cobbled alleyway while we contemplated ambushing our antagonists a sudden gust of wind made me look up at the stars. Fuming, Buck said, 'Don't ever fucking make me do that again! Ever!'

He put his hands on his knees and bent over double, retching. The briefcase never left his sight, on the floor next to his feet. The willpower necessary to restrain his fighting instincts had made him physically sick. And he'd done it all for me.

I got Buck as far as the Bar Luna, not exactly a gringo bar but not the sort of place that attracted the wrong type of Mexican like Rocinantes did. There were tables outside with white garden chairs, and inside was a dim, cave-like bar. Buck was still hyperventilating and started to explain that sometimes he just couldn't control these violent reactions, a hangover from Vietnam where anything that moved had to be killed. I plied him with more booze.

PRIMERA PARTE

UNO

It was midsummer and the court room's upper slit windows were open to allow the breeze through – the aircon must have been broken Buck thought – one of the windows slamming every few seconds making Buck jumpy. Subconsciously it took him back to Cuba twenty-something years ago, waiting for a troop ship; the noise of a loose shutter banging in the wind waking him up from a deep alcohol-induced sleep. Bang. Bang. Like a gun going off in the bedroom, the long white curtains brushing his calves and feet in the breeze. The grey slats reminding him he was in Havana with an aquamarine Atlantic ocean outside the window.

'Your honour we would like to call to the bench Major Buck Buchanan.'

The eerie silence in the court room did nothing to calm Buck's nerves as he saluted with one hand and raised the other to the proffered Bible. 'I do hereby solemnly swear ...'

'At ease, Major,' the judge interjected. 'This is a preliminary hearing. You will not be called upon at this time to offer testimony. Do you understand the charges laid against the accused?'

'Yes, your honour. I understand the charges.' He had sat bolt upright without blinking, eyes forward, as his friends' names were called out one by one accused of what the prosecution were calling 'heinous war crimes.' The list was an unappetising menu of human rights abuses; rape, torture, murder, sodomy.

Cold sweat ran down the collar of his heavily pressed uniform shirt. Every nerve in his body was screaming escape. His senses were on high alert; boxed-in like this he felt threatened and trapped and both his instincts and his training were telling him to attack.

Once out of the court room he hit the ground running and began his disappearance. Smoke and mirrors would be his best bet, he mused. The hearing was scheduled for 14h00 hours the next day, which gave him less than 24 hours to become invisible.

Earlier that day once Buck had left their apartment for his big day in court Carmen had started to prepare dinner. She would make a Mexican feast complete with homemade salsa, frijoles, quesadillas, guacamole and beef chilli. She had already started to chop the onions, tomatoes and chillies for the salsa and she had begun the frijoles, which would take most of the day to cook and recook and sieve and recook and sieve until she had the paste the way she knew Buck liked it. The kitchen smelled of fresh limes and fragrant coriander and onions and the chilli steam coming off the hob made her eyes sting.

The garbage disposal was refusing to do its job properly; normally this would be Buck's territory but as he was otherwise indisposed, no pun intended, Carmen picked up the phone and dialled their landlord-cum-curator, a Mexican she loathed for his sliminess, but she wanted the darned machine to work.

'Hello, Juan? It's Carmen, can you come and fix our waste disposal please?'

'Oh, Carmen. How can I reefuse such a beeyooteefull ladee? Reefuse, get it? I makee joke, yes?'

Carmen cringed at the hammy accent he always put on to try and be funny. 'Can you fix it or not?'

'Sí señora. Yes my ladee, I come efix right away.'

There was a knock on the door and Carmen wiped her hands on her apron as she walked towards it. She kept the chain on.

'Sí?'

'Sí, mi amor, soy yo. Eet ees me, Caarmenseeta.'

Carmen rolled her eyes, and let him see her do it, before taking the chain off and opening the door.

'Come in. You know where it is.' She went ahead to check on the pots.

'Jou sure you a Mexicana? I meena wid a elong elegs like a jours. Maybe jou a Merican preencess?' Carmen did not answer; she was used to Juan's bullshit.

'Oh, dios mio, but Caarmenseeta, it essmells deeliciouss!! Jour food ees a making me a hungry!!'

'Please just fix the garbage disposal, that's what we pay you for, isn't it?'

'Si, señora.' Juan lay on his back and shuffled underneath the basin, his bag of tools close to hand. 'Hey, I kinda likea the view from down here, if you know what I mean?' He laughed and set about fixing the faulty unit. Carmen rolled her eyes again and busied herself with the dinner preparation.

When Juan had finished he caught Carmen unawares, and grabbed her waist from behind while she was stirring one of the dishes. He kissed her neck. Carmen felt icicles run down her spine.

'Don't do that.' She said in a tone which hid her fear, but would have left any normal man in no two minds that his attentions were not warranted.

He stepped back and tried a plaintive face, 'Please Carmen, just a little kiss? I'm so lonely.'

She turned awkwardly and started to plan how she could get past him and run out of the apartment. She should never have invited this idiot into her house; it was her own fault. She thought about arming herself with one of the knives but remembered something Buck had once told her about people who wielded knives in a fight without knowing how to use them. She was lost and on the verge of panic.

Juan came closer once more and pulled her towards him, 'You're so beautiful, Carmencita.' She felt his beard as he pushed his face towards hers, and she turned her head to one side. She started to push him away with both her arms and hands, but he was stronger.

'Get off, get off!' she sreamed, 'Leave me alone, damn you, evil man!'

Juan maintained his tight grip with one arm and tore her tee shirt and apron with the other, revealing one of her breasts. The fact that he then cupped it and tried to put it in his mouth gave her the split-second necessary to kick him hard in the groin. After that she just ran, not waiting to see whether or not he was going to follow. She knew he was a coward and doubted that he would. Her moment of aggression had empowered her and she even thought about going back to kick the shit out of him. But no, she knew somebody else who would do a much better job.

If it was up to Buck he would not carry a cellular phone, preferring as he did to live off the grid. As far as he was concerned the less The Man knew about him the better. His wife made him carry one in case *she* had an emergency. He smiled as he pressed the power button thinking that she would no doubt make him wear a crash helmet if he ever got a bicycle. Buck had decided that he could no more testify against his fellow comrades and friends than he could sell his own mother to a pimp – if you weren't there you wouldn't understand. He dialed Wain's number from memory.

4

'Hi Wain.'

'Who's that, Buck? Wooh shit, you got a cell phone are you kidding me?'

'No need to wet yourself Wain, can you get hold of a car for me?'

'Sure, what do you need?'

'Something cheap, and reliable enough to get across the border. With the right paperwork.'

'How cheap are we talking?'

'Two or three hundred tops.'

'I can hook you up, brother. When do you want it?'

'Tonight.'

Both men were as good as their word, and they'd been friends for a long time. Buck ended the call but put the phone in his jacket pocket without remembering to turn it off. Carmen's call came through as he was transferring between stops on the subway. He stopped walking and ducked out of the fast moving sea of commuters and anxiously took the call.

'Hola, mami.'

'Buck, ayudame!'

'Mi amor? Que te paso?'

'It's Juan, I called him to fix the garbage…' Her voice broke up. She was garbling her words, and crying.

'Slow down, Carmen, take a breath, are you ok? Tell me what happened?' In fact he had already heard all he needed to know; Juan. If that slimy fuck had touched his wife it would be the last thing he ever did. 'Did he touch you honey? Are you hurt? I'm coming, ok?'

'Venga! Pronto…' was all she could manage before the line was cut. Funny, Buck thought, I don't use my cell phone for two years and now it's saved my life twice in one day. He made a mental note to destroy it and the SIM card as soon as he knew Carmen was safe.

Buck arrived at the apartment and having first checked Carmen – who was with her best friend and neighbour as he had hoped she would be – he went to look for Juan. Eschewing the elevator Buck took the steps one flight at a time heading towards the basement where Juan worked in the Apartment Complex Super's office-cum-utility room. Eight storeys (and sixteen seconds) later he spotted the unmistakable skulking shape of Juan trying to nip out unnoticed through the emergency exit to the underground parking bay area.

'First mistake Juan; you should have run when you had the chance,' Buck shouted and leapt over the remaining banister rail.

Juan dropped his duffel bag, produced a flick-knife from his sleeve and started to wave it at Buck. Juan was visibly sweating and he looked like the victim even before the fight had started. Even Buck gave him balls for trying to put up some sort of resistance, but it was a thought he quickly dismissed.

'That's your second, and last ever mistake.' Buck said as he involuntarily set his neck and back muscles to a position of greater defensive strength. His arms too locked into attack mode and his feet planted themselves in position. It was all automatic.

'So, you like to fight with knives, huh? Sure, you're a Mexican. I bet you think you're some kind of expert? Ok, so let's see what you've got.' Buck was buying time and scanning the car park for potential witnesses. Buck had already decided what was going to happen. His mind had been able to work fast even while he was flying down the twin flights of stairs. Juan would be killed and the body hidden. No one would look for him for at least a week. The car from Wain which was already earmarked for dodging the military tribunal was now going to take him and Carmen away from the murder – and the USA – for good.

The bays were all-but empty. It was still mid-day and people were at work. Juan was the day-time supervisor and residents had swipe cards which worked the barrier. They were alone apart from the security cameras. The cameras might be a problem but the feed, Buck presumed, went straight to Juan's office so he could steal or erase the tape if need be. It would be better though to get Juan back towards his cubby-hole.

Buck started towards Juan, 'I always knew you were no good, Juan. But this, hurting my Carmen? That I'm afraid is not forgivable. Make your move. Do your worst with the knife.'

'You think it's the first time I fucked your wife? It's the second time mother fucker.' Juan made a surprisingly adept leap towards Buck and tried to cut him in the back as he leapt over Buck and through the door towards his office. Going to ground, which is exactly what Buck had wanted him to do. Buck took one last look around before he quickly followed Juan, 'You should have run the other way, dude!'

As a practical man himself Buck was well-versed in the layout of the building's basement. He knew there was a gas-powered furnace that ran the central heating and hot water systems. A man could get through the service hatch which is where Buck was about to drag Juan's lifeless body, as soon as he'd squeezed the life from it. The next time any of the tenants opened a hot tap or turned up their heating the blue flames would start to destroy any evidence of Buck's crime.

In less than a minute Juan's knife clattered to the floor and Buck retrieved it and thrust it up into Juan's rib cage in one fluid movement.

'What do you think about that, Juan? You normally have so much to say. I guess you won't be raping any more women will you?'

7

*****

'Bienvenidos a Mexico. Welcome to Mexico.'

Six words which rang in Carmen's ears like rain at the end of a long hot day. She wiped the sweat from her forehead and replaced her hat and sunglasses thanking the border official who had returned their id's and waved them through. Buck was also relieved.

'Today is the first day of the rest of our lives, baby.' He reached across, kissed Carmen, put the car in gear and drove off. He threw out the toothpick he was nervously chewing and said, 'I don't know about you, but I could use a drink! There's a bottle of rum, and Coke in my bag. Do you mind mixing us one?'A wry smile crossed his lips and even a chuckle. Carmen began to giggle.

'I love you too, baby.' She said, lighting a cigarette and passing it to Buck as she started to rummage around for the drinks. 'Venceremos! Patria o muerte!'

Even the weather seemed to share their celebratory mood. Clear skies of hot white pearl and wide blue horizons filled with cacti-covered hills, hummingbirds and butterflies offered infinite possibilities. Buck's instincts had been correct so far. The authorities would still rely on him turning up for trial in the morning which gave him at least twenty-four hours and they were already over the border. Juan had no real family in the US and would not be reported missing for days if not weeks, by which time the charred remains would be extremely hard to identify. His suspicion was that he would get away with that one, but Buck was not one to dwell. He would do it again in a flash to anybody else who touched his wife.

DOS

I first flew to Mexico when I was eight years old. This is the last memory I have in which my mother and sister and I are happy together. Now that my mother is dead, the details seem important.

Drifting gently downwards in a giant bird towards the carpet of lights which twinkled beneath us like a sleeping beast's skin, I was acutely aware that we were entering a new world. I felt as if Mexico had tied a string to me, that the string was being pulled. There was nothing I could do about it.

We were booked into a hotel for the first night, Hotel Oxford, and we would then make our way to Acapulco by bus the next day. It was Independence Day and just round the corner from the hotel, the Zócalo was jam-packed with thousands of people. Mom was a bit of a hippie, so as soon as we'd settled in, showered, flicked through the TV channels – including a couple that we shouldn't have been seeing at that age – and unpacked we headed straight out into the mêlée. We were all hungry but Mom reasoned that it would be much quicker to get something on the street, rather than sit and wait in an empty Formica hotel-lounge hell.

So it is the traffic-cordoned-off, hot streets tight with people and the sensation of Mom's hand squeezing mine tightly, and my little sister's hand holding me that I remember. Eating mangoes for the first time. The giant floodlit palaces draped in flags. Mexican kids throwing eggs and flour at everybody. Street vendors selling umbrellas and eye-goggles to protect the crowd. The three of us eating tacos, hot dogs, corn on a stick with mayonnaise and paprika. Such a happy family.

Acapulco was its own adventure. The bus played movies which might have been straight from the hotel TV which made Mom blush and laugh. We drank soda and played I-spy out of the window. The beach was covered in sewage and trash flushed down the hillside by flash floods in a storm the day before we arrived. It was clouded over but not cold. Mom found Hotel California and decided we should stay there, because of the song I think. We drank coconut milk through straws straight from the coconut that was chopped by a nice man with a big machete. Mom even bought one for Sylvia, my sister, although it was almost as big as her. Mom never despaired despite the weather. The next day a whole team of trash-pickers moved along the miles of white sand dressed in white plastic overalls and yellow gumboots clearing everything neatly away into big orange plastic bags like something out of a nuclear holocaust movie. Even the sea, which had a nasty undertow, a ledge and powerful waves, didn't get us down, we paddled and laughed and ran along the beach and played Frisbee instead of swimming. At night after supper – in the hotel this time – we did long jump competitions in the sand until the waves washed away the record of who had leapt furthest. Before sleeping we were allowed to stay awake and look at the stars with Mom while she ran her hands through our hair and told us how special we were, and how much she loved us.

Mom died soon after we got back from that vacation. It was virulent breast cancer that had not been diagnosed early enough. I knew then that it was time for me to man up. I took it upon myself to look after my baby sister, and to protect her at any cost. I write this now as a grown man. My sister is fine. She's a nurse in a psychiatric hospital and doing well for herself.

My mother was never able to tell me for certain who my biological father was, but she had a few ideas; she was very open about that. Almost as open as she'd been when she was screening prospective sperm donors in the late 60's and early 70's. One of the prime contenders was a writer who'd retired to Mexico. The Professor. I tracked him down through his publisher and asked by letter for a paternity test but he declined – never denying that he'd known my mom, but reluctant as an old man to get involved in '[my] games' nonetheless. I was studying Mexican Literature at NYU and they were about to send me to the University of Guanajuato on an exchange program. I determined to at least try and look him up when I got there.

You can still pick out my house on any poster or postcard of Guanajuato. It's a big inverted capital Tee directly opposite the camera on the far side of the valley, above the university and just below the highest point of the ring-road or periférico. Over the years it has alternately been painted pink, yellow, and blue. The tower is not a tower at all just a way of housing and disguising the water tank on the roof.

TRES

The day Buck had been subpoenaed to appear in court and testify against his unit, he was sipping a Long Island Iced Tea in Cape Cod. The bar was familiar from childhood, and he liked it, sitting and watching the sea, getting drunk quietly. He had an aunt whom he never saw and was contemplating getting in touch with her when the man charged with delivering the sealed envelope and those immortal words 'you've been served,' popped up. An innocuous grey man, he seemed to derive fetishistic pleasure from his role in life. Buck read the letter, and lit a small hand-rolled doobie while the juke box played Steely Dan.

Buck squinted into the setting sun and crunched on an ice cube, the cola and alcohol working their magic. He would die before getting on the stand, simple as that. He would take Carmen back to her homeland. Mexico's acceptance of death as part of the ongoing cycle of life appealed to him. He'd seen the face of death daily in Vietnam. Living, eating and sleeping with the fear of death became a way of life. Well-trained as he and his comrades were, the heat and the chaos, plus the increasingly non-sensical nature of the missions they were expected to fly tended to push men into a realm of sanity that looked ok on the outside but was rotten on the inside. If they were the same physically they were never the same mentally after the war. That he had witnessed what members of a certain company did before they were air-lifted from a particular village was of no concern to anyone outside the war. If you weren't there, you wouldn't understand.

As a door gunner he'd just been doing his job when he noticed that something wasn't quite right. Buck's Huey was coming in low and hot to pick up soldiers from the LZ – which was routine. But he could see from the air that there were too many dead civilians. After taking off from the first extraction once he'd worked out what all the fragments of information were telling him, he ordered his pilot to go back down. With the rotors still spinning he got out, knocked unconscious a marine intent on executing a Vietnamese boy no older than five, and with the aid of his M-16 persuaded the perpetrators of the massacre to stop it.

After two days of driving slowly south they came across the pretty little town of Guanajuato, nestled in the middle of the Sierra Madre mountains. It spoke to them both. Less touristy and ostentatious than its more famous neighbour, San Miguel de Allende, Guanajuato had a certain understated charm.

'I love it here, Buck. You know when you just get a feeling?'

'Yes, I know, baby. I like it here, too.'

'Makes me want to start a family...' At this point, Carmen was gently play-punching her long term boyfriend (life partner) on the upper arm and ribs.

'You want to make a baby?' He grabbed both her wrists with one hand and pushed her onto the bed. She pretended to fight him as he tried to kiss her on the mouth.

Outside the sun was setting and soon the people of Guanajuato would be heading out for their walk around the local square in the jardín.

'Let's go and promenade with everybody else.' Carmen said it enthusiastically as though the idea had only just come to her, which it had of course. 'I want them all to know that we're happily married and going to live here for ever and ever.'

'Aren't you forgetting something?' Buck said as he pulled her closer to him by the hips, the sliding movement forcing her short skirt to ride up her thighs and reveal her crotch. Carmen wrapped her legs obligingly round her man's midriff. 'We'll need to practice if you want to make a baby!'

Buck took a deep breath and knocked on the door that might make him a university professor if he passed the questions put to him by the committee he imagined waiting for him behind it. His thoughts briefly turned to an older man – a Professor himself – who had taken an interest in a young pot-washer before the war. He smiled inwardly and pushed the thoughts aside. It was late afternoon and the sun was brushing its last rays of golden paint onto Guanajuato's green hills. Light flowed through the windows of the university's upper storeys and flooded the floor and walls with light. Buck was not religious but the golden glow had an effect even on him.

After waiting for two minutes he knocked again and got the distinct feeling that there was no committee. Curiosity got the better of him and he opened the door, summoning a, 'Disculpe, yo tengo una entrevista aqui a las seis…' in his best Spanish.

He found one Mexican girl seated in a chair (her black curly hair hiding her face from Buck) opposite a man who looked a little flustered on the other side of a desk, in the chair opposite with his back to the window.

'Si….si Senor,' the accent gave away his British expat origins. 'Dina was just leaving.'

'Hi,' she said, 'and bye.' Looking coolly at both

14

men she left the room and closed the door. Buck knew then and there that he had got the job. And, he allowed himself to fantasise, perhaps the girl?

So Buck got a job at the University of Guanajuato as a history teacher and he began to think very seriously about marrying Carmen and settling down. Before he knew it, they were married and pregnant. That's when Carmen wanted to decorate the nursery. And that's when Buck met Dina again.

He bumped into her in town one day painting portraits of tourists in the jardín.

'Hi, are you the girl that does the murals?' He'd already heard people talking about her and mentioned it to Carmen.

'Yeah.'

'My wife wants you to do one at our home.'

'Don't you want to know my name?' Buck was shy around her for some reason and she was quick to pick up on it, playing with him.

'Sorry, yes. I'm Buck, nice to meet you. My wife, Carmen, and I ...Well, we're expecting a baby and she wants, we want, to decorate the nursery.'

'Dina Martinez. Nice to meet you, Buck. Carmen is a lucky lady.'

'How old are you by the way?' *She looks about ten,* he was thinking. *Maybe I'm just getting old.*

'Ha ha, didn't anyone ever tell you not to ask a lady her age?'

Yeah, who taught you that, your dad? 'Ok Dina, it's your secret. No problem. How do we do this?'

'You work at the university, right? I'll find you.'

Buck stood still and didn't know what to say.

'It's a small town,' she said by way of an explanation and waved goodbye as a man on a motorbike pulled over to pick her up and sped off.

CUATRO

Boom! The thunderclap went right through Henry's skull, piercing his brain behind the eyeballs. Why are the mines dynamiting this early, for God's sake? Don't they know that some of us have only just gone to bed? Boom! Why are the mines dynamiting at the weekend? Boom! Maybe it's firecrackers at a wedding? Boom! Boom! He buried his head inbetween Dina's breasts and covered themselves with the one sheet he (they) sometimes slept under, his hand on her waist pulling her towards him. Silence. Then the dogs, the cockerels and the church bells all started up in unison to fill the void left by the end of the dynamiting. They both laughed. It was going to be a difficult hangover. Henry got up to be sick. Dina (bless her) rushed to the shop to buy cold milk for banana smoothies and started to make quesadillas. After breakfast they would go back to bed and sleep for a couple more hours before making love again, showering and getting up to go to work.

Classes at the university started at six a.m., much too early for Henry who was usually coming home from Rocinantes at that time. But not too early for their friends Jenny and Buck who both taught there. However, the tiny town he called home was never more beautiful than in those early hours around dawn when she first opened her eyes. This is when he felt most Mexican and could think and even converse with himself in Spanish. Feeling alive, feeling loved – he picked his way through the cobblestones with purpose, deftly avoiding the darker corners where men, dogs and even horses had pissed the night before. He wondered if hookers had even fucked there despite the stench and realized he was probably horny.

Days, weeks, whole seasons flew by like clouds in timelapse photography. Now the steps were muddy with tufts of grass and running with rivulets of rainwater, now they were hard, dry, slippery, polished by passing feet and hooves. It's easy to fall in love when there's nothing to do. There's no need to decide what to wear because you already know you're going to put on the same cut-off denim shorts, boots, and blue tee shirt as yesterday. The biggest decision you might make is which shop to buy snacks and water in before you climb out of town to go hiking. White flour tortillas and oranges. Your daily routine allows you to embody the free spirit which lies at love's very core – you are at one with yourself and your surroundings: There is no need to carry water because you drink it from the stream. The stars light your path at night and do away with the need for a torch. Money for beers after work is received that same night in tips, making a wallet redundant. You float on the wind because you can and are not bound by an alarm clock or watch because the sun shining through your broken glass window wakes you up; unless it's the beating of the rain on the tin roof, or the shifting hips of your lover as she starts to stir.

CINCO

Buck was born to poor immigrant parents. His dad was a shunter on the railways. At nineteen Buck was working part-time washing dishes and writing poetry. It was a phase. At 20 he was a door gunner in Vietnam.

The young Buck was something of a loner. Not a sensitive kid who was bullied, but a self-confident individual who swam against the tide and didn't care too much for what anybody else thought. He lost his virginity at fourteen, to his thirteen year-old sweetheart, Rebecca. As next-door neighbours, they had already loved each other for close to ten years.

A split-second traffic accident took Rebecca's life. Buck was there and nearly lost his own life trying to save her. His face, chest and arms were badly burned as he pulled her body from the wreckage but the long hair and moustache he's sported ever since cover up most of the damage, and the burn scars you can still see look like acne pock marks to the casual observer.

Aged nine, Buck was the head of his small family unit. His poor parents both became ill with Polio and looked to their only child to provide care and support. Buck's father could no longer manage the physical aspects of his job with the railroads and he had to stay at home. As a shunter he was obliged to wield a hefty hooked stick, but more than that it was the split-second timing necessary to flip the heavy chain links from one carriage to another that meant the difference between success and failure in the shunter's yard. Long goods trains in particular were a demanding mental and physical workout, the window of opportunity was literally a split-second as boxcars came together onto their buffers and the compressed chain sagged momentarily; which boxcar is going to which depot, over and over. His father started to drink, and carried on drinking after the death of his wife – a suspected suicide. Buck had had enough and left home. He told his father that he would get a job and send money for him, but only on condition that he stopped drinking. It broke Buck's heart, just as it had broken his ma's, to see Pa like this. The man who had risked everything to come to America from the troubled Balkan state that hadn't yet become part of the new Europe and was not yet on everyone's lips as it produced super models and tennis players. The man who had built the house they lived in with his own bare hands.

Buck finished work as normal – it was a Friday – and headed down the three hundred or so steps from his office to the nearest hole-in-the-wall bar. He allowed himself one caguama while he smoked and watched the world from a long-legged plastic stool. He still had on his corduroy jacket and was carrying the leather briefcase which those who knew him knew never left his side. He was trying to remember if he'd seen anyone between here and there selling flowers? He would walk to the jardín, buy a bunch of flowers and then try and get a taxi underneath the square where they were allowed to pick people up in one of the tunnels. In the cab he didn't feel inclined to say much and once through the tunnels he was happy as he watched the sky open up and the hills rush towards him like so many giant toads or frogs, the mountains that gave Guanajuato her name.

'Dígame, Guanajuato, where is all your silver and gold?' he said under his breath, smiling.

At home the nursery had become a studio. It would seem they had a visitor. The furniture and floors were all covered in white sheets and in the middle of the room was Dina; a mess of black curly hair painting a circular sun right in the middle of the wall. She was adding red to the orange glow and completely alone in her own world as Cuban guitar music played on a portable cassette player that must be hers because it wasn't his. She felt his presence in the doorway and jumped up to say 'Hi,' throwing both her arms around his neck. For a split second he was enveloped in the smell of paint and ptuli oil and *Teen Spirit* roll-on deodorant. He remembered the flowers that he had bought for Carmen – his pregnant wife – and somewhat awkwardly (for him) went off to find her.

There followed a short period of calm, although Buck found himself idly wondering whether he'd ever be left alone in the house with Dina? While he should have been busy teaching, Carmen did her thing in the house, Dina painted and Buck went to work. The mural progressed nicely.

Buck had never been unfaithful to Carmen. It had never crossed his mind, and he didn't want to start now by having sex with this young girl. However, Dina had already decided that they would have a love affair and once this seventeen year old had made up her mind, there was very little anyone else could do. Carmen went away to see relatives in nearby Leon which pretty much put paid to all efforts by Buck to suppress any animal urges he may have been feeling towards the teenage artist crawling around all day semi-naked in his house.

It all started innocently enough (the seduction): They shared coffee, beer, and the occasional spliff. They talked about music; about art. But one day they kissed and it quickly stepped up a notch to a whole other level of intense love making, all orchestrated by her (unbeknownst to him).

Once the mural was finished, she cut him off cold. He was destroyed for a couple of weeks but soon after that his first child was born and Buck's life-focus changed. Circumstances allowed him to forget her.

One day Buck came home from work to find a man in the kitchen holding a knife to his wife's throat.

'Where is it?' the intruder demanded.

'Where's what?' Buck countered. He splayed the palm of his left hand as a sign for calm as he gently made to lower his briefcase in his right hand.

'Tu cara. The máscara. The mask.' Then, almost as an afterthought, he added, 'Fuck with me and she gets it in the neck.'

'Please there's really no need to harm my wife. The mask is right here, in the next room, let me show you.'

The assailant was caught in two minds and momentarily relaxed his hold on Carmen. Buck caught her eye and motioned with his eyes for her to duck. Just at that moment he flung the heavy briefcase at their attacker's head and his knife clattered to the floor. Buck sprang on top of it and plunged the blade into the man's ribcage and heart. 'Again,' he found himself thinking in quiet disbelief. The stranger fell dead to the floor and bled onto the terra cotta tiles.

Buck didn't really register that he had now killed two people as a civilian. He thought quickly and decided that he would need a pickup truck to drive the body out into the hills. Aldo, one of his pupils, drove an old truck which would not arouse suspicion on the streets and he knew where he could quietly borrow (steal) it from him without being noticed. He quickly left the house on foot, lit a cigarette, and went straight to town through the tunnel which connected his cerro with the town centre where Aldo's family had a print shop. The walk should have taken thirty minutes but he did it in twenty and was driving back in the old Ford jalopy before he had even had time to think about what he was doing. For Buck it was all about training, protecting his family, and professionalism; don't get killed, don't get caught.

Buck wrapped the body in two old sheets that Dina had been using to protect the floor from paint. The cargo was not visible to anybody seeing the vehicle drive past once it was loaded into the back.

Buck had been out to the presa on his bike a couple of times and he figured that he would find a good hiding place in the hills. He wanted to go further than the dam, though, and took the road past it, and the old mine, up to where the sierra madre began to spread out in all of its desolate majesty. He wasn't too keen on driving there, given that the vehicle's tracks would be easy to find, but had no choice. Perhaps he should have scouted a hiding place first on the bike? But no, that would have meant leaving Carmen at home with the cadaver. Buck parked at the foot of a high and sheer rock face which seemed to have caves at the foot of its final escarpment. He turned the engine off – marveling at the silence – and went to explore on foot. As he approached the cave mouths he turned around and took in the breathtaking view of the valley below. He suddenly felt quite high up and wondered if Mexico had mountain lions or cougars that he should worry about? Then he remembered that it was jaguars he should be fearing in these parts, it was good cat country. The cave entrances were small and apart from a few feathers, bones, and animal droppings, looked undisturbed. Unfrequented recently by people that is. One or two marks on the higher inside edges looked like ancient rock art, and Buck wished he could explore properly on another occasion. If the caves were ancient sites, somebody would probably know about them and come back here. He preferred to drive on to a smaller, more forested hill.

The hillock also looked promising but wasn't really big enough. At least that's what he thought until he found a seemingly bottomless sink hole. He'd have to be strong to throw the body past the overhanging tree roots, creepers and flowers but he would give it a try. Buck bravely balanced close to the edge of the drop on an overhanging rock and tossed the body out in front of him. The deceased's feet bounced off one boulder near the top but the body then plummeted head first into the darkness. Buck never heard a splash but imagined there was one eventually. He thought that even if cavers came here to abseil they would have a hard time tracing the body back to him. It would just be another dead Mexican gangster.

Nearby there was a little abandoned church that he and Dina had visited a few times and he took a drive over there.

From time to time the demons came back and Buck was haunted by memories of Vietnam and what he had done and seen. At times like this it was impossible to get through to him. You could stare into his eyes and see that he wasn't there any more, that he was back in Nam. You had to be either very brave or very drunk to get this close as being throttled by Buck wasn't out of the question.

At the end of the third and final tour, leave in Saigon was a difficult time. There was elation, they had lived through a bloody war and seen many friends killed in action. There was devestation; the one unanswered question, WHY? Would keep popping into their heads. Of course, there was no answer to that one. Why had so many people had to die? There was euphoria; they were young and Saigon was a place where anything went, especially then. There were plenty of girls. They were US-dollar-rich. It was lawless and they were ready to get laid, get high and get drunk. Mostly though, it was an energy-sapping come down from the adrenaline and constant high alertness of battle. The paranoia that set in with doing nothing; being idle in cheap hotels, arguing with staff, fighting with each other. It was hot and they were racked with guilt when the alcohol wore off. It was better to stay drunk. One officers' mess occupied the first floor of a once-grand hotel in the centre of town. Marble columns, crystal chandeliers – that kind of place. They spent a lot of time there, drinking, flirting with the girls and waiting for passage home. As well as the local pimps there were black market traders, carpetbaggers who wanted more from life than the few bucks that the girls and the gambling brought in. One hawker in particular worked on Buck – who spent slightly less time than the others downstairs getting his dick wet – consistently imploring him to come and see something 'very special indeed. You like. I promise.'

Buck finally caved in the day before they were due to sail home. It was one last throw of the dice at getting drunk on Cognac and French Champagne. Across the roof tops he could see the sun setting on the sea and life suddenly seemed like something to be taken hold of and lived the hell out of. In short Buck had an epiphany and told himself never to overlook another opportunity again so long as he still had breath in his lungs. Aviators on, cigarillo in teeth, bottle in hand, he followed his friend downstairs and went through a back door to a little alleyway where old iron fire escapes like liana vines dipping into the Yangtze came down to meet trash cans. Behind a bead curtain into a neighbouring building – smaller and less grand than the first, the back of a service laundry Buck guessed – and from there into a tiny ply-board walled room lit by one naked bulb with a bed in it.

'Fuck man, I didn't come all this way for pussy!' Buck exclaimed and was about to walk out.

'No, please. Is my house. You welcome. You take

seat.'

Buck's host reached under the bed for a box that was wrapped in a blanket. He laid the box neatly on the bed next to Buck.

'You ready?'

'You bet,' replied Buck.

With the box open Buck was a little taken aback. There was no doubt in his mind that this artefact was genuine. Stuff was turning up from all over the place. But this ... he knew he had to have it.

'You like? You pay five hundred dollar!'

'Don't fuck with me, man. This piece of shit ain't worth squat. I'll give you a hundred. Because I like you.'

'Is still five hundred. No problem. I ask other GI.' He closed the box and started to wrap it back in the blanket. Just then a slim lady came in through the tiny doorway. His wife – Buck could tell at a glance – she was sweet and pleasant looking.

The host said something quickly in Vietnamese 'go away, we're busy' type thing, and there was an awkward silence. Buck took a bunch of notes from his breast pocket and counted it out in front of his friend. It came to $410 dollars.

'All I got, friend. Take it or leave it ...' Then it was smiles all round and there were even little tea cups suddenly to drink Sake and Champagne from.

And so Tezcatlipoca's mask became Buck's.

SEIS

The Professor was just about to exit his front door and had one arm inside his jacket when a tall young man with nervous good looks and tousled hair approached him. It had to be Henry. He pulled the door to and locked it, carefully putting the key in his pocket.

'Good morning. Bit hot for a jacket isn't it?'

'No, I don't think so and it's the only way I have enough pockets to keep everything in.' He patted the pockets of his trousers, waistcoat and jacket mentally going through their contents. 'You know we never used to have to lock the doors here.' The Professor said wistfully.

'I would like to talk to you if I may.' The boy automatically touched the hair behind his ear.

'Yes, of course you do. I read your letter, Henry. It is Henry I'm assuming? Perhaps we should have coffee first? I know a great place.' The Professor smiled and patted Henry on the back trying to make him feel less awkward. 'Let's walk out together into the sunshine shall we?'

'You mean the place you go every day for coffee?' Henry asked.

'Ha ha, yes. You've been checking up on me, asking around? Good. When you get to my age, routine can become not only necessary but also quite beautiful; even poetic. And I'm a bit late today. I hope they don't give my table away.'

'They wouldn't dare do that, would they?' Henry had indeed found the Professor via the café staff who served the old sage every day at around 10.30 a.m. every morning.

'Um, probably not. Well I hope not.' The Professor looked genuinely worried for a moment. 'Did you know Neal Cassady stayed here before he wandered off on his last walk?'

'Yes I knew that. Do you think Kerouac and Ginsberg also stayed here?'

'No, I don't think so. Cassady was here without them, later on. But he meandered off and fell down dead on the railway tracks somewhere not far from here.' He was getting distant again.

'I'd love to go and find the exact spot. You met Kerouac, right? And Ginsberg?'

'Let's get to the café first and then we'll talk properly. Where are you staying, Guananjuato you said?' The morning sunlight was golden on San Miguel's brightly coloured walls and doors as they continued down the centre of the cobbled street. There was a strong smell of wet dust as housewives and maids watered hanging plants and emptied buckets after cleaning. Henry noticed that no one was saying hello to each other, perhaps it was still too early.

The zócalo was a beautiful colonial square flanked by two large churches with twin towers. Artesanías were busy laying out their souvenirs and Henry sensed a lot of colours, smells, sounds that were subtly different from Guanajuato where he was staying. He liked Guanajuato better but didn't know why. For breakfast and the day's first coffee The Professor took them to his regular haunt on the corner of the main square where he could quietly watch everyone. First they had to buy the international version of yesterday's Times – which he always received a day late, and its arrival determined what time he would go to the café. Lunch, dinner, tea all had their own different and equally secret cafés and restaurants. For drinks it was a whole different story with another complex logarithm to determine where and when based on moods, company and level of intoxication required. There might also be the factor of The Professor seeking company which would take him away from the erudite-middle-class expat scene completely and into a more insalubrious collection of callejones and rincones.

Today, the paper was on time and they found his usual table free which seemed to visibly lighten the Professor's mood. They ordered coffee and huevos rancheros and then he turned to Henry, 'You were asking about Kerouac? Sure, back in the day. But I never met Neal.'

'It was more about Lowry for you?'

'Old Malc, sure. A great percentage of the people in the world haven't had this experience, but sometimes you read a book – for me it was *Under the Volcano* – and it's almost as if that book's been written for you, or you're the only one who really understands it. The impulse – creatively, artistically, spiritually – was to say, 'Be my daddy. Be my father.' It took a letter or two, but obviously I struck a chord. He had done the same thing. As a young boy in England, he'd written to Conrad Aiken, he so admired Aiken's poetry. I became friendly with Aiken, too, through Lowry. When Malc died, we got back in touch, and when he was in New York he would come to dinner. He kept a cold-water flat – are there still such things? – up on the East Side.'

'You also became friends with Dylan Thomas and Kerouac?' Henry was loving the eggs and wondered if he'd ever find a way to broach the subject of the reason behind his own Mexican odyssey.

'The Dylan Thomas thing was a fluke. I don't

think I'd ever met a writer. Back then, I was only in correspondence with Lowry. Thomas did a reading, and on impulse I went back stage. You can't imagine how popular he was or how highly thought-of he was, even though he was a legendary troublemaker. Out of the blue, I said, 'How would you like to have a couple of drinks with some graduate students?' He said, 'Yeah, I'll meet you.' One thing led to another, and we had, at most, nine or ten evenings together.'

'So how did you meet Jack Kerouac?'

'Kerouac was sheer chance and non-literary. My next door neighbour at the time, on 11ᵗʰ Street in the Village, was a recording engineer, and he was friendly with Jack. They used to listen to jazz together. In fact, this guy, who's long-since dead, was one of the first to lug that old-style heavy equipment up to Harlem to record it. Jack loved it, and he'd go with him once in a while. He lived right next-door. Frequently, we'd go from apartment to apartment drinking together. Sometimes, Jack would come to New York, and this fellow, Jerry, would be away, so he'd ring our bell. For about two years – I'm guessing a dozen, fifteen times – the doorbell would ring, never a word in advance, and there he'd be, drunk as hell all the time. Generally he'd stay the night. One time he borrowed a tee-shirt. He came back a week later, and we're sitting in the living room, and I'm recognizing the outer shirt from a week before. I saw this filthy T-shirt and said, 'You son of a bitch, is that the shirt of mine that you put on here a week ago?' And he said, 'Well, I had a shower.' Then he stopped coming around; I guess he was in Florida. We just lost track of him, and the next thing I knew he was dead.'

There was a pause, during which Henry nearly said something, but he was mindful not to break the Professor's train of thought and they both sipped their coffee. The eggs were much better than the coffee Henry thought to himself. After some seconds the older man continued, on a different tack.

'I was reading something the other day about Tezcatlipoca. Yes, something about a funeral mask which once made it all the way back to Spain with the conquistadors but was then stolen – ransacked from a palace or somesuch during the time of the Moors. Scholars and treasure hunters are suggesting that some of this evidence is as much real as it is anecdotal. A trader in Vietnam came forward and says that he sold a similar object to a US Marine in the 1970's. So it's possible that this mask still exists, in the hands of a private collector.'

'What does the mask represent?'

'They say it is more than symbolic, that it has special powers. But there seems to be something of a curse like with Tutankhamun's treasure – those who come into contact with it meet funny ends. It's a good story.'

'Where did you read all this? I'd like to see the article.'

'I can't remember what I was reading. You can ask Arturo at the ranch; it's the kind of thing he gobbles up.'

After coffee Henry was free to explore San Miguel. He found the railway tracks and followed them for a few miles, thinking about literary fame, the nature of fiction and the course of his own life's journey; could the Professor really be his father? It got hot and without much shade water became a priority. He planned to head back into town and cool off in one of the swimming pools but he remembered there were none that he'd seen, and opted instead for swimming naked in rock pools and streams along the way; something that would become a necessary feature of future walks in and around the mountains of Guanajuato. Refreshed but still a little bit dizzy he headed back into town at dusk, and suddenly felt very thirsty. As he approached the main plaza the Professor beckoned him to come and join him at his usual (evening) table in the jardín. Not the same café where they'd had breakfast, this was a restaurant he favoured during the week for dinner. In yet another routine, dinner at the weekend was back in the ranch where he stayed, because the Professor found the jardín far too busy and unbearable at the weekends.

'I prefer to drink, and dine for that matter, *sans plebs*, if you know what I mean? That's why I always book such an early table. How was the walk?'

'Good, thanks.' Henry thought the Professor must be quite well-off to be able to afford this lifestyle.

'Beer or wine?'

'Beer please.' He really wanted water but was too embarrassed or sun-affected to ask.

'One Corona for my friend, and a bottle of white wine for me please. Better make it two Coronas, por favor. Actually, they're *Coronitas*. Another reason not to drink here too often!' The Professor laughed. 'Hmm and please bring a jug of iced water! That's for you, young man.' He half-waved the fingers of one hand as if thanks were not necessary. 'It's the food I like and the view of the people in the square. What do you know about duality?' The Professor seemed half-cut or perhaps a little-too-lively and Henry noticed a cigar butt already in the ashtray as he lit another one.

'Is it something to do with ambivalence? Love-hate kind of thing?' Henry was busy helping himself to iced water and the peanuts, which were already on the table, for much needed rehydration and salt.

'No, I mean duality as a central theme in ancient and modern Mexican society.' The Professor prepared to light a cigar and asked rhetorically 'Do you mind if I smoke one of these?'

'You mean like pluralism?'

'No,' he puffed, 'pluralism was political. This is cultural. And religious.'

The alcoholic drinks arrived. Henry switched to another beer which came in bigger bottles and ordered two more; with fresh lime. He lit a Winston Light.

After asking if they could look at the menu, The Professor continued, 'That's what it's all about, Henry. The whole beauty of life in Mexico. The philosophy of dualism.'

'You don't mean pistols at dawn?'

'Nope.' He laughed and blew smoke into the evening air.

'Two of everything?'

'Ha ha. Again, no. Although that's not a million miles away from it. Everything exists side by side with its polar opposite. Life and Death. Old and New. Love and Hate. Take Day of the Dead as an example. For one day of the year families are able to communicate with their deceased relatives. But, those same relatives are here with us every other day of the year, just that it so happens we can only communicate with them on November 2nd . The whole country is dichotomous, starting with Mexico City. The modern, Spanish city is literally built on top of the foundations and ruins of the ancient city. They coexist. So it is with belief systems. Catholicism exists side by side with many beliefs and gods from the ancient Aztec and Mayan worlds.'

'But all the festivals and Saints' days are purely Catholic, aren't they?'

'On the face of it. Yes. Are you hungry? Next time you're in Mexico City you should look up Tezcatlipoca, Lord of the Smoking Mirror. He's a very interesting chap.'

*****

Witnessing the Professor's daily routine in San Miguel was like going back in time, it felt as if Henry had stepped into a Mexican realm that co-existed with the expat life he had only so far seen, but remained hidden. The relationship was not symbiotic. This life continued regardless, with or without the other one. The Professor had immersed himself in the comings and goings of an old hacienda where he rented a room. He lived with vaqueros who spoke and swore in a thick dialect barely resembling Castellano, who drank hard and worked hard all day in the fields. Most of these men still marked their names with a cross in the wages ledger at the end of each long week because they couldn't write. It was a cocoon, a moth that would never see the light of day. Or maybe it would? Maybe the creature would grow wings and eat its way out of this tourist-trap town, taking a few of the tourists and expats with it? The walls of the main house were thick and pock-marked from bullets fired during the revolution. The heavy table was stained dark as much from blood as from the century of elbows that had lent on it, and the edges were scarred deeply from spurs that had sat there on tipped back chairs and blown cigar smoke towards the ceiling rafters. Maybe bullets would fly again, just as they still did when the men were drunk and shooting into the air for fun? Maybe the women and children would come back, the walls that once rang with laughter and screams from newborn babies would again fill this void?

But the Professor was not complaining. He quietly studied the camaraderie of these stoic, agrarian men, and admired their strength as they woke up before dawn and spent the whole day with the sun on their strong backs, broad shoulders and heavy-set beards and eyebrows. They accepted him, but he knew that he would never become one of their brethren. Nor would they ever openly divulge that one or two of them could occasionally pleasure him. They accepted him, and that was enough.

To him it was a welcome retreat. It allowed him time to think. He had tried living with various friends in the expat community but there was always far too much inane socialising, there were far too many women. Too much cunt, and not enough cock.

At the hacienda he had found peace. The Professor had one small room full of reference books and notebooks. His bed was a mattress on the floor. He had a collection of spent shot-gun cartridges picked up during long walks through the surrounding hills and woodland. So the daily pilgrimage to town was just to enjoy the best coffee, and get the paper. Today it was the *Austen Chronicle*. Tomorrow it might be the *New York Times*. He was teaching, and still writing, but only poetry. His last published contribution to the prose novel was 1988's *Chagal's Widow*, a masterpiece of postmodern deconstructivism that still made it onto academics' and aesthetes' top-ten lists.

Mexico in the 1970's was Mecca for the Professor. As a poet he knew well that Hart Crane had commited suicide by jumping ship in the Gulf. That Neal Cassady had died on the railway tracks somewhere outside San Miguel. It was a trend that began with B Traven's exploits in the 1920's. Traven himself had disappeared into the mists of the Mexican jungle spawning many rumours. Malcolm Lowry had then done his level best to single-handedly build and destroy all self-destructive myths in one anarchic, towering novel which was his *Under the Volcano* masterpiece. The Professor was intrigued and the rest is well documented but the two became friends and the Professor wrote his own Mexican contribution called *Going Down*.

So what did the Professor think about Henry, and his visit? He wasn't sure. Age had mellowed him and whilst he could still play the Playboy he wasn't libertarian or anarchist enough to ignore the fact that he might be the boy's father. He just hoped that such a sensitive soul wasn't going to be sucked down into the enticing maelstrom of ancient Mexico's counter culture – which he now remembered he was responsible for introducing Henry to in the first place. He lit a cigar and allowed Paolo (one of his boys) to pour him some more red wine. The sun was setting from blood orange, to ochre, to umber, and crows, which the professor always viewed with disdain and fear, were fighting pelicans (who always heralded joy) for perching rights on the Professor's roof.

*****

The Professor had not had a normal upbringing; father going to work each day, mother at home baking. His father was a painter and scrap-metal sculptor, which meant that Dad was home all day. Mom on the other hand drove a motorbike for her own Wall of Death show, which joined various circuses throughout the year, and meant she was on the road a great deal. The fact that the Professor wrote poetry from a young age didn't really bother his father but he always had encouragement from his mother. It was about this time, when he got his first spectacles, that he earned the Professor epithet. Mom was bisexual – or just plain lesbian according to Dad. The Professor joined her on the road from time to time. Driving long distances between towns, eating junk food and meeting strange folks up and down different county lines. He marvelled at his mom as a strange leather-wearing lunatic who chose to hurtle horizontally round the inside of a wooden barrel rather than stay at home with her husband. The marriage was not working. Even as a kid he could sense that.

He published his first book fresh out of high school, and after his father's decidedly underwhelming response, hit the road and didn't go back for twenty years, until the old man had suffered a stroke and written him a post card to come. Pop had remarried in the interim – a pretty black girl – and explained to his son that he'd always been proud of him, but never knew how to say it, as he had felt like such a bad father. A lot of it was down to financial stress, and once his art had finally started to find a market with buyers he found himself alone with no wife and no son. Samantha had started out as his secretary then slowly she'd moved in; helping him to tidy up, washing, cooking, and finally they'd fallen in love.

The young Professor was living the dream. His left-wing mysticism was suddenly in vogue, and it felt as if he himself was the centre of a cultural and spiritual revolution. It was the 60's. He found himself rubbing shoulders with several literary giants, such as Dylan Thomas and Jack Kerouac but his personal passion was for Malcolm Lowry, the reclusive author of *Under the Volcano*. As an undergraduate the Professor wrote to his hero, requesting an interview. Lowry was flattered, both as a writer, and as a confused homosexual. The young Professor followed him to his remote cottage in Canada. There was much laughter, pipe smoking and whiskey drinking. Even the wife came on to him which was a little awkward. They canoed to the pub each evening over miles of deep and potentially life-threatening icy water.

The professor had first come to Mexico on a pilgrimage. He'd found his own Quauhnahuac (Cuernavaca), in the shape of San Miguel. He simply loved all the flowers, and the pastel-painted doors, cobbled streets, the unabashed *machismo* of the men. He warmed to the thrill of Mexico City, and bought an apartment there.

No. 309 Rio Lerma, was a spacious apartment with four bathrooms and six bedrooms. If he was famous in San Miguel, it seems the Professor was equally as renowned in the big city, which despite its size was just another playground to him. The night Henry was invited coincided with a party for a local newspaper editor that was so well-attended when the police turned up to shut it down, they couldn't get in. The apartment was definitely on the map. Henry remembered tucking into red wine then white wine followed by vodka. When the beers finally ran out he was sent to get some more, only to return two and a half hours later (by which time the Professor had organised a search party to look for him), having had several large whiskeys at a place called the *Bar Inglés* in the middle of the Zona Rosa. The *Bar Inglés* was wall-papered in tartan and sported a large pair of antlers on the wall. All very Scottish. Henry asked the barman which English beers they had? None. Which English cigarettes? None. So what was so English about it, he asked? 'El ambiente.'

SIETE

For an hour before sun-up and an hour after it even Mexico City is a quiet capital, in the air the thudding rotor blades of helicopter commuters builds in the distance nowadays but on the ground it is a giant that wakes slowly, you suspect as it has done for thousands of years. Now is the time for lovers who slept in parks to face the real world – him in a once-clean dinner jacket and her clutching heels too uncomfortable and too high to wear sober. Street cleaners marvel at the sunrise on clear days revealing the statuesque beauty of a city ALL THIS TIME protected by twin volcanoes, each and every man and woman's father and mother – all twenty million of them. The homeless start the day early, dragging giant plastic sacks filled with tin cans that might yield a few pesos at the recycling plant. Taxi drivers head for bed while others are polishing their bonnets and rims ready to do battle with the mean city streets.

Watching such scenes from his hotel window in Reforma, Tezcatlipoca allows himself a few seconds of contemplation on behalf of mortals like Henry who only know this one fleeting existence and takes another swig of his beer.

The light of day gives vague sunshine through the smog but no city heat. The Revolution Monument towers above me honouring Francisco Madero, Lazaro Cardenas, Pancho Villa, Obregon, Calles, Zapata. I find a café in Calle Edison and order breakfast – café americano with a torta de queso – I wolf down the complimentary pan dulce's. The four-lane highways are slowly filling up with VW Beetles and US hand-me-downs but the city (twenty million strong) is still sleeping. The weather, dictated by el smog – is hazy but not hot yet.

Chapultepec Park, the lungs of the city is where I go to find real Mexicans, people not concerned with hustling, or robbing, or busy with the rat race. History sits quietly here amongst the palaces and the trees. I sit and eat my cheap triple-decker sandwiches, listening to the traffic and watching a family picnic that turns into a fight for no apparent reason. It starts to pour with rain. Later, while I'm having my hair cut round the corner from the museum of anthropology, a woman with all the authority of the owner's wife comes in from the rain to have her trousers blow-dried with hair dryers.

The tiny local buses to the ruins of Teotihuacan, the ancient city, are an adventure in themselves. No trip to the bus station is complete without an inspection of the latest sci-fi, bull-fighting and real-time police-crime comics; or a cling wrapped sandwich with one green jalapeño placed delicately on top. It seems like an initiative to improve on the western custom of putting the gherkins inside the sandwich; whether you wanted them there or not.

Trotsky's house in Coyoacán with its preserved study – the stage of his assassination – was always a must-see as was Frida Kahlo's house, with her mesmerising collection of paintings. The house in Guanajuato, which I'd already seen, where Diego Rivera was born hadn't been able to secure such fine examples of his work. Trotsky's house, hidden on the edge of a busy six-lane highway. an unassuming monument to a moment that changed world history forever. Trotsky and Kahlo were lovers as well as neighbours. Her diaries speak fondly of his Russian penis.

The murals of Siqueiros and Rivera together were beginning to colour my subconscious. Regular visits to the anthropology museum, the pyramids, the floating gardens, plus unlimited access to the Professor's library meant that I was steadily immersing myself in Mexican mysticism, if not mystique. Nights in Guanajuato, Leon, San Miguel were spent drinking. Nights in Mexico City were spent reading.

Coatlicue, the Earth goddess, gave birth to warring twins, Tezcatlipoca and his sister, Quetzalcoatl. Tezcatlipoca took it upon himself to not only try and kill the rival twin but to also off his own mother, thus becoming the undisputed number one god. As the lord of smoking mirrors he is life and death, love and hate all rolled into one, equally as capable of planting a flower as he is of reaping destruction on a whole city. He is the jaguar, he is eternal youth, he is death itself. It is this lord of darkness who began to breathe new life into my hollow skull. More precisely, I began to understand that much of Mexico's soul – if that's the right word – rested on his pillars of duality. That the obsidian mirror was with us in the here and now just as it was with us in the ancient past. Just as the temples still stood, so too did some of the philosophies. Lord of the near and the nigh. Possessor of the sky and earth. He by whom we live.

Indeed, early attempts at conversion to Christianity by the conquistadors failed until they hit upon the notion of painting Christ and the crucifixes black to trick the native Mexicans into believing that Tezcatlipoca had returned. Yet in truth, once Tezcatlipoca had escaped through the gardens of Macchu Picchu to the higher sanctuaries only the gods knew about, he was able to sit and watch as human folly unfolded itself beneath him, ever grateful that more blood was being spilled in his name.

The more I saw of Mexico, the more I liked it. The professor's flat in Rio Lerma gave me freedom to explore the capital and I walked it, day and night, and took the metro to all four corners. Rush hour was of course impressive and intense, especially at the biggest underground train stations where millions of people can converge on the trains in minutes. Here the platforms are segregated by armed guards to stop women getting molested. Chapultepec park is enormous. Likewise the university, its campus effectively a small town with its own buses and taxis. Insurgentes is the biggest street in the world. Yet, despite all this, the constant smog, the constant traffic, the constant threat of robbery, there are daily pockets of calm where the city's streets are empty and quiet. As if the metropolis can also sleep, and can also take a siesta. Dawn in the parks when street sweepers and bar and shop owners come out to slake the pavements with water and settle the dust. Calm periods in the giant bus stations, when even the beggars and pickpockets are just thinking about coffee and breakfast. Seconds spent sitting at a juice stall, or eating tacos by a drinking fountain or drinking beers and eating tapas in a bar, moments of escape. The frenetic energy doesn't dissipate to Coyoacán – still a rich enclave. The slums don't even begin for another two hours' drive out of town, beyond the breweries. There are calm moments on the floating islands of Xochimilco where you are not bombarded by hawkers and mariachis. There are minutes before the rush hour begins with its trucks and trains and helicopters when the night is perfectly still. Breaks in the smog when the clouds reveal the volcanoes and you can see and feel the mountain air is as it once was. Between tourist groups in the national palaces there are moments when you can study the murals alone and feel their intensity for oneself – I already felt a certain empathy with Rivera as he was born in Guanajuato, and I'd visited his house. I was open to all things Mexican and they came to me.

*****

      He who would have seen the Aztec empire in its prime, should have stood, about the beginning of the sixteenth century, upon some pinnacle of that mountain wall which fences in the matchless vale of Mexico; from such a height he might have seen the fair lake of Tezcuco, that miniature salt sea, and the fresh tide of Chalco the sweet water, with other bright sheets of silver, shining along the valley for seventy miles. Into this vale the Aztecs descended in 1325; they had wandered from some far country to the north, and having borne a thousand toils, saw at last, upon the margin of lake Tezcuco, a fair omen, which told them that their pilgrimage was finished; it was an eagle holding a serpent in his claws, as he sat upon a cactus, or nopal. Here, amid the reeds and upon the salt marsh, they laid the foundation of an empire, which, in an existence of three hundred years, rose to the pitch of occidental grandeur with a rapidity unparalleled. Upon the islands of Accocolco, whose bog-like character required them to bring stone from the main land, they planted the first rude huts which were to shield that homeless race from the opulent tribes around, into whose territory they had penetrated, and upon whose terra firma they were not allowed to rest. Years of privation, misery, and hardship, rolled by, and the huts of the wanderers became safe habitations, and handsome houses: the miry marsh was now the firm foundation for solid superstructures, and the arms of the Aztecs had made the name of the poor wanderers among the water-flags a thing for terror and respect. By the beginning of the sixteenth century their sway extended from the Atlantic to the Pacific, from the region of the barbarous Otomies upon the north, to the farthest limits of Guatemala upon the south; their language was spoken by seven tribes in and around the great valley; they were the Sochimilcas, Tepanecas, Colhuas, Tlahuicas, Mexicans, and Tlascalans; the latter tribe threw off their allegiance, and repulsed by repeated defeats, the other six tribes, and established themselves as an independent republic, some seventy miles from the city of Tenochtitlán, or México, where they remained the rivals for years, and ultimately became the cause of the final overthrow and downfall of the Aztec power.

It was a glorious view from the mountain heights to see this Eden-like valley surrounded by a chain of porphyritic mountains, whose purple heads in the distance, through the unclouded atmosphere, seemed to lean against skies of pure ultramarine; far away to the south-east Popocatapetl, though distant more than thirty miles, shot its shaft of snow, like a shining spear, high and glittering into the bright blue skies; and hard by his side, in her spotless shroud of a thousand years, stood Iztaccihuatl, the white woman, his silent partner, who with him overlooked the land; the speechless watchers of centuries in their flight to eternity!

*****

The more I read about Tezcatlipoca, the more convinced I became that my destiny lay with his (was mixed up in the religious philosophies that seemed to make so much sense to me). My mother had brought me here to Mexico for a reason. I was here again for a reason. Each year the sacrificial victim was chosen just as the outgoing incumbent was executed. It was a great honour and families put their male children on the waiting list to join the priesthood from birth. For sickly children it was a good way of being productive outside the fields, where their lack of physical strength would have been a hindrance. The lucky chosen one lived as a king should for a whole year before his death, attended by four handmaidens or ceremonial wives. On the day of death, he carried himself to the top of the high steps where the priests and soldiers took him and tore out his heart with an obsidian knife. The victim's blood was as grease which oiled the great wheel of the sun, and kept all life in perpetuity. Tezcatlipoca himself would then greet and guide his newest recruit through the tunnels that

43

connected this world to the next, and he alone had the power to grant the boy's next wish; would he choose to die right here and now and enter the spirit world? Or choose to live in between in servitude of the king, and frequent both the spirits and the earth, fulfilling anything that was asked?

*****

In the eighteen months which composed the Mexican year, there were human beings sacrificed in each one, saving the eighteenth or last month, which commenced about the first and concluded about the twentieth of February. There were various forms of sacrifice, and the offerings to the different deities varied in their character; the chief objects, however, were human beings, rabbits or leverets, and quails; and of these birds the multitudinous numbers offered exceed all belief. One of the most singular ceremonies was the sacrifice to the god Tezcatlipoca; this victim was the handsomest and best-shaped youth of all the prisoners; they selected him a year before the festival, during the whole time he was dressed in a similar habit with the idol; he was permitted to go round the city, but accompanied by a strong guard, and was adored everywhere as the living image of supreme divinity. Twenty days before the festival, this youth married four girls, and on the five days preceding the festival, they gave him sumptuous entertainments, and allowed him all the pleasures of life; on the day of the festival they led him, with a numerous attendance, to the temple of Tezcatlipoca, but before they came they dismissed his wives. He accompanied the idol in the procession, and when the hour of sacrifice was come, they stretched him upon the altar, and the high priest with great reverence opened his breast and pulled out his heart. His body was not like the body of other victims, thrown down stairs, but carried in the arms of the priests and beheaded at the bottom of the temple; his head was strung up in the Tzompantli, among the rest of the skulls of the victims which were sacrificed to Tezcatlipoca, and his legs and arms were dressed and prepared for the tables of the lords; after the sacrifice, a grand dance of the collegiate youths and nobles who were present at the festival, took place. At sunset the virgins of the temple made an offering of baked bread and honey.

The festival was concluded by dismissing from the seminaries all the youths and virgins who were arrived at an age fit for matrimony, the youths who remained mocked the others with satirical and humorous raillery, and threw at them handsful of rushes and other things, upbraiding them with leaving the service of God for the pleasures of matrimony; the priests always granted them indulgence in this kind of youthful vivacity.

Close to the great temple were the public schools, with distinct departments for male and female, noble and plebeian students, where a Spartan education was given to them physically, and their minds imbued with the precepts of their religion. At the end of every fifty-two years there was a grand festival of rekindling fire, which element they superstitiously believed would be lost to them without this ceremony. A procession was formed of many miles in length, which, headed by the priests, wound its way to a neighboring mountain, where after offering up a sacrifice, renewing the fire upon an altar, and immolating their victims, who were generally prisoners of war, the multitude returned to the city, and a general Bedlam-like Saturnalia took place, in which, breaking all their crockery-ware, and beating their wives, cut the most important figure.

*****

I soaked it all up. It was full of sex and gore. Bodies tumbling down staircases, virgins offering themselves and their lives. Multitudes breaking plates! But always the underlying POWER of Tezcatlipoca's unquestioned, unwavering rule.

The real victory was won underground by Tezcatlipoca, who had forced the crusaders of the cross to desecrate their own most powerful symbol in order to pay homage to *HIM*. They had painted their precious crosses black. I saw it all so clearly. It was then that I started to see visions. I had become a holy warrior. In Mexico City waiting for a bus to Tenochtitlán, an old woman sat begging with her husband. She tugged my arm and forced me to make eye contact, not unusual for a persistent beggar but there was something more. Her toothless mouth made no sound more audible than grumbling. It wasn't Castellano and I suspected that it may have been Quechua, Nahuatl, or some other form of ancient Mexican no longer spoken by most people. Using sign language she asked me, no commanded me, to bring them food and drink. This was to be my moment, I felt as though I had a direct line to the ancient Mexico I was falling in love with. The gods walked among us; I was convinced. The husband lay asleep and looked for all the world like the most pathetic figure imaginable. How and why she would continue to care for him was anybody's guess? I dutifully bought them sandwiches and coffee, and excitedly delivered my manna. The sparkle had gone from her eyes and she hardly recognised me. The gifts were received grudgingly. Had I bought the wrong thing? Whatever door had opened in her soul was closed again. She tore at the plastic wrapper, and inspected the contents of each sandwich. She ate both chillies, and gave one sandwich to the sleeping man. She dipped the flimsy triple-decker bread into her coffee. I was crushed, yet blessed. I knew it was the beginning of better things to come. I would never again ignore the plight of those Mexicans with nothing. These were my people now. The street sellers, the pedlars, the mime artists, taxi drivers, pickpockets, strippers. Priests, nuns, choir boys could all go to hell; my god was older and fundamentally more important than theirs. The stage was set for whatever was about to befall me. King for a day. I had tasted it and wasn't about to let it slip away. It was a blazing awareness. I was blind but I could see. Asleep, yet wide awake. Alive, but dead.

He by whom we live.

*****

Weeks were spent in penetrating these interminable forests, and winding with his troops and allies through the mountain defiles and fastnesses; now in the scorching rays of the sun of mid-day and again in the chill air and rain-like dews of the nightfall; now marching in the pure sweet breezes of the hills, and again shivering and hiding for shelter from the pitiless peltings of the storm-blast, as it burst from the mountain cloud, and ran roaring through the forest, beating and drenching the unsheltered band, whose brave leader, defying the might of the elements, suffered all without complaint, and wore a front so bold and dauntless that the haggard and despairing eye caught new life from its glance, and the fainting form pressed forward with an invigorated step, as his bold and thrilling voice bade them be of good cheer, and have firm faith upon the Virgin, who would watch over them in their perils, and never desert her children who bore on the cross of Christ!

Cortes could not sleep, would not sleep again even with his head on Malinche's breast. Victory had come at a bloody price. Only after he himself had charged a stunned enemy on his horse was he able to turn the tide of the battle. He was not prepared for the scale of the slaughter, for the might of the mass-sacrifice. Ten, twenty, thirty thousand cut down in their prime, almost charging the swords as they protected the Emperor with their lives. Cortes could not command such courage amongst his men; professional soldiers on horseback with superior weapons. Hailed as a bearded god, Cortes understood that he had, on this day, relinquished any claim he may have had to be a real Christian. His life was over.

*****

Like others before me I began to see alcohol as a way of getting closer to this netherworld of the gods. Tequila, mescal, pulque all had connections to the earth and allowed the drinker to communicate with the other world. Pulquerías had traditionally been off-limits to women, as Tezcatlipoca looked only for male servants to carry out his duties. But Quetzalcoatl might recruit women...

As my visions increased in their intensity, I knew that when the time came, when I would be called upon, that only peyote would open the last remaining door to that world where I was destined to carry out his bidding.

A recurring dream: That woman in the desert, my whole mouth numb and then my feet, my legs – my whole body fizzing gently, focussing my mind on the sunset, riding towards them, standing stock still, maybe just the flick of her scarf unfurling. I see her left profile, her sunken eye closed, her dark beaten skin. The third figure is obscured but clearly hers, her son. The right eye is fine, black like her hair, a damp well full of tiny, tiny white shells – as she breathes, the skin is drawn across her left cheek bone to open a long scar-like razor slit, revealing the second eye, too low and lifeless beneath this wall of taut rubbery flesh, a shiny, new-born conch, winking...

*****

A snake slithered away into the wet jungle and Henry was left in no doubt that the drugs they'd been taking were starting to affect him. The sky seemed to be on fire and everything turned purple and gold. Except the red flowers which continued to grow in size and comfort him. Blue and green humming birds flew in and out of the scarlet petals spreading pollen. All the metal surfaces in the house lit up like bronze as the day's last rays loomed large and beamed deep bathing rays to drown them in perfect Mexican light. Henry struggled to speak. He wanted to tell the Professor about his feelings for him, and how it didn't really matter whether or not he was his father, but simply having introduced him to the ranch bla bla bla. The room still spun and flies, or were they cicadas danced in the dying light.

Henry's lips were as heavy as his jaws and he was only able to sit and stare. Fire filled his eyes and then his soul. In a way that he had never experienced before, he left Henry looking at the sunset and started to explore a hitherto unseen world in between this one and what he now knew was the gateway to the next. But he didn't go alone. His guide, he knew, all along, was Arturo, the Professor's butler who had told him about the lost treasure.

'Are you Tezcatlipoca? Henry asked, simply.

'No. You will not meet him until you are ready.'

The hallucination finished as soon as it had started with a crash and Henry heard the Professor's housekeeper asking again, 'Cerveza, señor?'

He blithely accepted and then reflected after the first sip that he had never felt so good. He tried to iterate how much but the Professor interjected, 'Feels good, huh?' Somehow it didn't sound like the real Professor but he accepted only what his eyes could see; the Professor and Henry sitting across from each other by what suddenly felt like a very small wooden table. Had it been weeks, or was this still today, just a drink after dinner?

'Where is everyone else?' Henry asked.

'It's just the two of us.' He passed Henry a lit cigarette, and pushed the bottle of tequila towards him. 'Here.'

OCHO

Living in Guanajuato is like entering a Gothic candy store through a secret tunnel. When I first arrived, after a long bus journey with two Mexican B-movies – *Dangerous Summer* and *The Phenomenal Thief* – I got a room in a crooked hotel run by a hunchback who always wore a curly wig. Painted in two-tone blue my room felt like an empty municipal pool. I say crooked hotel because it was squeezed inbetween two other buildings and had been constructed with no straight lines – not a single right-angle in sight. They had a full suit of armour in the lobby's stairwell.

Cervantino ran into Day of the Dead: One arts festival celebrating the life of Spain's Luis Cervantes blending into a cultural celebration of the after-life. It was non-stop. Night blurring into day, only to yield to night's charms again. I didn't sleep. I didn't have to – the bars didn't close. I marvelled at how a city already at the bottom of a valley had expanded underground, exploring Guanajuato's extensive and intriguing tunnels.

I dined underground in a small restaurant which overlooked one of the subterranean streets, serving the best hamburgers in town. The bread was doughy and sweet and the patties oozed grease and while I was broke (before I ate every day for free at the restaurant we opened – Chicago's) I could scrounge one of these from the orchestra guys who usually ate there. The restaurant window was a large ventilation grill which gave much needed fresh air to the tunnel below. It was romantic to eat above a narrow callejón which disappeared under an arch so close you could touch it and to look down into the city's underbelly.

The coolest house in town was clapboard and pale blue; the three-storey, twin-turreted Casa de las Brujas – or House of Witches. The occult never seemed far away in those early days. The first 'witch,' Isabelle, was never into magic be it black or white. She was merely a local girl whose one and only true love had made her rich, and when her husband passed away she grieved traditionally; wearing black day and night until the time of her own death.

They met in secret and holidayed in Barra de Navidad where one of her masters, a rich mine owner, had a beach-villa. The story of how they got their money is, and always was, the stuff of myth. Buried treasure? Stolen silver? It broke her heart, they said, when her husband died and left her childless with a big old house. She wore black as a viuda (widow) but was never a witch (bruja). The clothes were enough to start the rumour on their own. Her husband was a friend of El Pípila himself, the hero who defended Guanajuato's citadel of innocence against tyranny and unwittingly started the whole Mexican revolution; in which Isabel's only son had died fighting, they said.

Guanajuato was a boom town, and Isabelle was one of its princesses. It was a city of golden dust and orange blossoms. At the weekend labourers came in from the fields to spend their wages, riding into town on white horses wearing their best white clothes to get drunk and go whoring with women who sang gypsy songs and flashed their petticoats and gold teeth. The narrow, cobbled streets lent themselves to romance ... Exhausted miners would also wend their way downhill to the city on payday to buy enchiladas mineras, eat tacos, get drunk and visit the same prostitutes. These were halcyon days, the women just as sweet as the pulque that stuck in their men's beards.

So it should really have been called Isabelle's House or the House of True Love, but the locals jealously nicknamed her a witch for her wealth and her widow's garb, and the Gothic architecture helped the nickname to stick.

The expats who lived there nowadays were mainly American and usually came from money. There would always be the odd Jeep or Land Rover in the courtyard and horses were kept for guests who knew how to ride. If celebrities were coming into the Sierra Madre to escape the bright lights of the D.F. or the cameras of San Miguel they would come here. If by some fluke we ever attended their parties, they would want to know how and why, and who had given us access? They were all artists or artistes with tenuous links to success and fame. Individual bedrooms led off three sides of the first-floor courtyard away from the blue wooden hand-rail and tiled walkway. The fourth side was open to the sierra, and beyond the fountain and tall eucalyptus that was the view. Guanajuato's famous hills like so many Indian chiefs, or gods, sitting in silent judgement with folded arms. All seeing.

Even with the doors wide shut it was never quite clear who was actually inside each room, doing what, or with whom? Doors would close slightly on approach. Even to get an 'in' to be allowed to chill there during the day was something of a mission. If, like me, you weren't into smoking dope and could think of nothing more boring than hanging round pot-heads all day, it was no big deal.

NUEVE

Tezcatlipoca pushed open the door of the diner and was hit by a wall of cigarette smoke, the smell of recently cleared-up sick and Sheryl Crow piped through the speakers. As he took two steps inside, the smell of food also reached his nostrils; eggs, bacon, alcohol, yellow cheese, there was soda, coffee and burning bacon. And strawberry milkshake. The door was one of those plush bright-red affairs with padded cushioning and a port-hole window. The dining room was bigger inside than it looked from the street − one central kitchen-bar-serving station with booths dotted all around it. The décor was pure generic kitsch. Out back were the pool table, juke box and rest rooms. It was busy for this time of day, but then the lot was full of long-distance trucks with wagon trains all waiting to get laid, get fed or get papers to cross the next county line and get paid. The kind of place where the waitresses were lifers and chewed gum; had the specials menu memorized and didn't give a fuck.

Coffee was placed in front of him almost before the Lord of the Darkness sat down. 'Cream?' Shirley asked, milk jug at the ready − Tezcatlipoca had read her name badge.

'No thank you, Shirley. Say, were you here maybe ten years ago? I had one of the best club sandwiches with banana smoothie I've ever eaten and I want that again please.'

Shirley stopped chewing and was about to utter a put-down when she was transfixed by the reptilian glint in her customer's eyes. 'It could have been me, I'll see what I can do.'

Had he willed it Shirley would gladly have given him her bush but Tezcatlipoca was here on other business. He glanced at the local newspaper's sports pages as a strikingly virile sixty-something woman slipped into the booth opposite him.

'Fancy meeting you here, brother.' Tezcatlipoca looked up but was not amused. He took a swig of coffee and met his new companion's glance, contemplating what to say.

'I like America. You look well.'

'It has its merits – if you like blind and blinkered people.'

'I would have thought those people were right up your street.'

'Thank you for coming.'

'It was the least I could do after so many years. Turning up, I mean. But don't expect to win this one.' Tezcatlipoca was hungry now and looked round for Shirley.

'I have seen it.'

'Yes, maybe you have but right now it is on its way HOME where you will never find it.'

A sprightly but wizened brother and sister sitting in an American diner somewhere near San Francisco had seen many moments like this. The brother had seen, and overseen, more death than he cared to mention. He thought about the tunnels under Guanajuato as he looked deep into his sister's eyes, they were like bottomless pools of dark water and he felt himself drawn ever closer to their edge.

Out loud she said, 'Are you ok my dearest friend

and brother? You look a little off-colour?' And telepathically, 'You were always weaker. It is time to surrender! Give me control of both worlds. You should hang up your boots in a whorehouse somewhere.'

*****

Boom-boom; boom-boom; boom-boom! The high Andes rocked to the sound of apprehensive drums. Tezcatlipoca, the King of the Incas, was feverish to the point of exhaustion, and languished amid ornate cushions stuffed with humming bird feathers, his nostrils filled with the scent of a thousand Calla lilies. Such a palace should not have existed in the high Andes. From afar the turrets appeared to be mountain peaks, each one a portal into underground tunnels and chambers unknown even to the occupants of the city.

The scene unfolding beneath his eyrie was symptomatic of an empire in collapse. The emperor's drummers summoned a war council but it was too late to fight the Spanish now; at least to fight them yet again and win. The new strategy revolved around hiding as much treasure as possible, preserving their culture for future generations, and pushing as many women and children into the higher, hidden refuges, while the remaining warriors would undoubtedly be called upon to sacrifice themselves. Indeed the exodus of people to the mountains had already started.

It was time for Tezcatlipoca's great festival and he would watch as a young man gave his heart and lifeblood just as they had year after year for so many centuries past. The Lord of the Smoking Mirror would feel his energy returning. And he needed it. Cortes had proved to be a somewhat worthy adversary. Yet he had Cortes' number, his spy Malinche had seen to that. It was more his people he felt sorry for. They were, after all, mortal.

Macchu Picchu was a hive of activity...beside him on one cushion more ornately embroidered than the others, decorated with fine gold thread and painted with gold leaf, was an object that imbued the wearer with untold powers. It was, essentially, the gateway between this world and the next. Tezcatlipoca was a god, a shaman and seer of visions, he himself had no need of the mask. Yet he must guard it from his enemies (who were many) and therefore place it personally on the face of each new disciple that they might also see through the darkness. The point of Tezcatlipoca's tongue protruded slightly through pursed lips and his eyes seemed to slit so that he momentarily resembled a Komodo dragon. The hand-maidens had caught his eye and he chuckled to himself that each year his chosen disciple should be tended to by so many virgins. They paraded past him now, naked, and in single file so that he could take in their firm outline and smooth skin. In his delirium he suddenly thought 'where do they all go, now that they are no longer of service?' And then he remembered that the ones he chose would go to his chambers, while others would be asked to stay on in the palace and groom hand-maidens for next year's sacrifice and others still would be allowed to go back to their families. One or two would have the honour of spilling their blood along with the young man who had deflowered them. Yes, now it all made sense.

Part of the ceremony's trickery involved the mask which lay at his right arm on the ornate cushion. Placed on the victim's face just before the high-priest cut out his still-beating heart with an obsidian blade and held it high for all those present to see, the mask would transport the sacrificial disciple's soul thus saving his life. He would then begin a new life of eternal servitude, becoming one of Tezcatlipoca's foot soldiers, traipsing the corridors of time and haunting each and every cynic and doubter caught in the twilight between this world and the next, and recruiting them.

Tezcatlipoca stood and admired himself in the full-length mirror that he had just stepped through. In order that he should blend in, the norms of the modern age demanded that his human form be more handsome than he was used to in centuries past. Admiring his nakedness, mortal thoughts of copulation stirred in his loins and he let go a wicked laugh as he remembered the sweet victory of conquest, a physical pleasure denied all those in the hinterland where existence transcended the corporeal, to a more spiritual level. First he would enjoy himself in the slums of Mexico City, before heading over to Oaxaca where he had some unfinished business. Emerging from the catacombs beneath the city's Anthropology Museum – an aptness that he enjoyed – Tezcatlipoca quickly found a staff room and put on the first clothes that fitted him, a pair of jeans, sneakers, and a tee shirt.

The city smelled just as he remembered it; not quite as he had created it, but nevertheless the humans had done much to rebuild his capital since the earth quake in 1986 that had prompted his last visit. Tezcatlipoca lamented the fact that he now had to come in search of human sacrifices himself, gone were the days when the temple steps and streets ran with blood in his name, but he was a patient man and could adapt. He knew that capitalism, Catholicism and Christianity could not last forever.

Tezcatlipoca spat as he remembered Cortes and that whore of his, Malinche. Whore that she should choose the white impostor over him, her excessively virile lord. How alike the groans of love to those of the dying. He shook his long hair from side to side as if to banish such awful thoughts, the memory of a different time, where Huitzilopotli and Quetzalcoatl had challenged him for supremacy. The tip of his tongue emerged between his thin lips at the thought of all that blood.

Meanwhile the 3, 000 year-old man was horny as hell. He was also hungry and found a suitable kiosk on a nearby corner. He ordered tacos and a fresh papaya juice, and started to work his charms on the two girls serving him. A third lady came and stood next to them and ordered her lunch and within minutes all three were in his hotel room, taking it in turns to administer to his every need just as it had been with his courtesans when he ruled his empire in person.

As gods Tezcatlipoca and Quetzalcoatl hadn't exactly had a normal childhood. Quetzalcoatl was Tezcatlipoca's brother but there was no real love lost, both wanted the same thing – absolute control over the entire universe. The old world, that is the pre-Columbian world had had its charm but was now dead and buried to both of them. The wave of corruption and vice ushered in by the new order was seedier, was addictive, was beautifully flawed in a way that only old men enjoying the taste of junk food could understand.

Buck was not really a sacrifice to Tezcatlipoca, he was a game, a rite of passage for Henry to kill his best friend. For Henry to realise the NEED to kill his best friend. Just another tossed skull tumbling down the pyramid steps. Tezcatlipoca stretched out on his water bed and changed channel with the remote. He'd ordered out, and pizza would be here any minute. The girls from the taco stand had gone, but two more girls were on the way as he'd asked the señoritas at reception to run to the liquor store for him, to get beers and Bourbon.

*****

...and in an hour not a sound was heard, saving the night breeze flapping the reeds of the latticed windows, through which the white moonbeams crept and threw their long lines of light upon the

marble floors of that now silent and deserted banquet hall.

So he went to the woods to do penance, and had a hut made for himself of green boughs in which he took up his abode, giving strict orders that it should be kept green during his self-enforced sojourn there; and he announced that he should subsist upon raw corn and water, and would remain until the sacrifice of Tezcatlipoca. Four other priests who lived in the temple of Teohuacan dressed themselves like the poor, and reduced their food to two ounce corn cakes and a mug of corn porridge daily.

DIEZ

The smack and scrape of stone on stone was only audible to those at the coal face. Five or even three meters distant from where the sixteen men dug with fervour, sweat dripping from their broad backs and dark eyebrows the silence was deafening, and the black all encompassing. Two slit-like green eyes glinted through the gloom and were gone again, as if deliberately glazed over. Seconds later the first blood-curdling scream was hurled at an indifferent wall of stone and less than an hour later all sixteen men lay dead or dying amongst the spoils of their mining – an insignificant pile of silver – and a sated jaguar licked its lips. Tezcatlipoca still remembered that day, as he did all others that held significance for him. The death of the miners had been necessary to protect a secret underground entrance to a tunnel that allowed gods and their acolytes to pass undetected from one part of the kingdom to another as if by divine magic. Maintaining the illusion was paramount. To the men that mourned it was a tragic accident the blame for which could be laid squarely at the feet of the conquering Spaniards.

SEGUNDA PARTE

ONCE

Almost overnight, a new shop sprang up right round the corner from Chicago's in a little plaza that I hadn't noticed before. But Guanajuato was like that, there were alleyways and streets both above and below ground that remained unexplored until life took you in that particular direction. My friend Drew, for example, lived somewhere behind the main market – a purpose-built concrete affair complete with tables, benches and market stalls like an off-the-peg market mould – towards the railway station where there was a plethora of juice stalls, taco stands and bars that tourists and many residents would never see.

From Austen, Drew was blonde and slight, but wiry. He had clean-cut good looks and impeccable Texan manners. Drew was the only non-Mexican contender for the state championship boxing title. He invited me to the gym. I'd never sparred before but soon found that it was a welcome outlet for pent-up angst. I liked punching people in the face. I also liked the pain of being hit. So, all in all, quite an eye opener. Drew had enviable skills both in the gym, and in the ring. I couldn't keep up with him in training let alone spar with someone of his calibre. But I could hold my own with other beginners. I used my height, and reach, to good advantage and soon found that speed made up for what I lacked in upper-body strength. I knocked out a young Mexican pretender with a well-placed left jab, and loved it. The next volunteer, a bit older and stockier – I imagined he was a butcher – walloped me in the eye and gave me a bloody nose, but I pummelled him on the ropes and gave him a couple of bruised ribs for his efforts.

I missed Drew's State Championships final and only found out later that he'd done exceptionally well, not only because he'd had to overcome the prejudice against him being the only white contender, but also because he was carrying injuries from a mugging the night before. Nothing short of heroic, in other words.

Drew came from a rural Texan background, he was a cowboy who had grown up riding any number of Brahma bulls, barebacks, saddle broncs. Bull dogging steers was his idea of a normal day on the farm. What I'm trying to say is that he just did things because he could. Or, if he hadn't done it before, then that gave him all the more reason to get his head round it and do it well. Becoming the only white boxer in this part of Mexico was a bit like that, it was just something he could do because he'd put his mind to it. Most people would have been put off by the obstacles – the bureaucracy, the racism – or the beatings, but he was unperturbed. If we went out to get drunk, he would stay home to work out and get fit; if there was a girlfriend tucked away somewhere I never met her and never heard him talk about it. That side of his life was kept very private.

The new shop was an art gallery, and *artesania* store run by Buck's wife, Carmen. I got an invite to do the bar on opening night and had persuaded Drew to join me. We were a bit late starting because I'd spent the afternoon with Toni the pizza chef, who was having problems at work. Sonja, the young chef he was banging, whom Dave referred to as Maria-Teresa which he thought was hilarious, had taken an overdose of painkillers in an attempt to kill herself, and we had rushed her to hospital.

Damage limitation meant making sure that her parents never found out who was responsible for getting their sixteen year-old daughter pregnant in the first place and trying to ascertain whether or not she was in the mood to tell them. There was a lot of up and down in Toni's cousin's taxi, drinking Bohemia's (never my favourite beer) from plastic bags, stolen from another cousin's bar. Thankfully Sonja was pulling through, and didn't seem to be the suing type. She still loved Toni too much.

Carmen was hot, 30-something with well-defined cheek bones and long legs. Buck was not in attendance, he had elected to stay at home and babysit. I found her incredibly attractive and quite formidable. I think I'd bought Buck's whole stance that she was something of a dragon; yet anyone strong enough to handle him could manage just about any situation. Mike was also at the party. I didn't let that bother me, as I was here for Buck, and of course I now wanted to impress the sumptuous Carmen. Mike seemed to be some sort of 'muscle', which was a little bit incongruous at the opening of a local art gallery and artesania shop. Was he a bodyguard? A business partner? Carmen's lover? I ruled out the latter option, my jealousy wouldn't allow it. Whatever his role, Mike looked different, and not only was he not perturbed by my presence, he appeared to not even know who I was. His eyes, and consequently his whole face, had changed. His whole demeanour was different. I knew it was drugs, although I had no experience of class A's. I didn't know if it was coke, or heroin, or crystal meth, or ketamine, and I didn't really care. Drew was a straight-laced Texan and chewing tobacco was the extent of his recreational drug knowledge, and knew even less than I did.

Rumours in this part of the world, were considered true. Perhaps it wasn't peculiar to our expat community? Perception was reality. The rumour about Mike was that he had been a very successful musician – a star – but that his drug habit had ruined his career. He was on the run from his past. The job in the orchestra was just some sort of front. Mike had his own bunch of shady henchmen with him. Mexicans I'd never seen in Guanajuato before, wearing clothes which put them firmly in the Mexico City income bracket. As Drew and I poured drinks, crushed ice, refilled glasses and lit cigarettes, I watched Carmen for signs that she was involved with these guys. Did she know them? Were they friends? Did she approve? But she gave nothing away the whole evening. They were there, Mike was too fucking high, and no-one seemed to care. We all ignored him and it's funny how instinctively nobody said anything despite the collective intrigue. Carmen spent the evening being charming and professional. I'm not sure how many paintings she sold but I think the event was worthwhile.

There was a power cut and we played the musical instruments that were there on display by candlelight until the sun came up.

DOCE

Dave had his own vernacular, a type of Spanish which left little to be misunderstood yet bore no resemblance to the language spoken by everyone around him for the past fifteen years throughout Central America. Looking back I think it must have been a deliberate ruse.

He disarmed customers at the door by waving his fat arms and shouting 'Pas-a-lan-tay, señor! Pas-a-lan-tay!' 'Pase, adelante' would be an acceptable, and formal greeting; one of respect, meaning 'please come inside.' Pas-a-lan-tay meant nothing, but the arms and the smile said it all. 'Me gusta pollo?' Was a question for many occasions. Literally meaning, 'do I like chicken?' Dave wanted it to mean 'do *you* like chicken,' or 'would you like some chicken?' but what it really meant was 'will you fuck me for some free chicken?' or if an official was being addressed, 'look at me I'm so stupid, I couldn't possibly be the gringo who's trying to fleece you and your government, could I?'

The other word that he knew in Spanish was *pechuga* for breast, which gave him countless opportunities for titty jokes that tickled him immensely. Unfortunately for Dave *lechuga* means lettuce, and he would often find himself grabbing one of his own breasts and pointing, saying to all and sundry, 'me gusta lechuga?,' 'do I like lettuce?' The locals took him with a large pinch of salt. Staff survived by resigning in quick succession.

Happy days, sober days, were paradisal in their simplicity. Everyone – expats, students, friends – always met first thing in the jardín. Teachers like Buck and Jenny would already have done two hours' work in the university by the time layabouts like me wanted breakfast at eight. We ate at Pingui's where we were always assured the same sullen reception however often we ate there. Instant coffee, huevos rancheros, frijoles, green salsa, freshly squeezed orange juice all served in or on the finest brown plastic tableware. From Pingui's we might saunter through the jardin itself for a bit, maybe buy smokes or a newspaper from a kiosk, and say hello to whoever was around. Pretty much everyone made it on to the 'say hello' scale, some more than others, obviously. Occasionally the bandstand would have a band in it. If we didn't buy a juice or an ice cream at the juguería and eat it on one of the benches under the box-cut laurel trees, it would be straight to the theatre steps where all of the students sat to pass the time of day and look at the jardin, and any other friends or students not already on the steps. Morning hunger pangs could normally be taken care of by a bag of caramelised peanuts down towards Tortas la Pulga and the railway station, or if one of the other Americans was around, at Daylight Donuts up by Rocinantes. The street kids here had a ritual of pretending to rob the store for the armfuls of yesterday's cakes that they were given for free, running in shouting and screaming 'esto es un robo!'

The centre of town wasn't only foot traffic. Private vehicles were few and far between but there were plenty of taxis and large, old-fashioned buses like yellow school buses in the States, which lumbered and spurted diesel fumes through the picturesque city centre with its raised pedestrian curbs, facilitating run-off of flood water into the tunnels originally dug to divert the river in spate but now used to ease the flow of traffic. A second, underground city. The theatre housed the state capital's municipal building and the regional jail which made it the perfect focus for anyone with an axe to grind, thus Catholic saints' days, name days, and national holidays were usually marked by a strike or a protest outside the theatre. This effectively clogged the traffic in the city centre but there would still be a subterranean flow.

After donuts or peanuts there was still time to kill pre-lunch, which meant either walking down to the old market by the train station - for window shopping and souvenir buying – or up to the Correo a few blocks behind the jardin to check mail and maybe visit the university or at least venture as far as the university steps. Lunch could mean anything from a homemade family feast of spaghetti, homemade banana bread, ice tea under the trees at the Mormon ranch, a walk towards Bel Air and a vegan chickpea 'treat' in a converted mansion (the real treat), set-lunch from chipped tin bowls at the local market by the train station (long bench tables or bar stools at the high counter tops, bowls of soup and beans with tortillas and salsa), but my favourite was always Tortas la Pulga, a tiny one-roomed affair selling the best toasted sandwiches imaginable.

Young as we were, siesta was anathema to us, so a walk up to the Bufa might be in order or if there was no evening shift, a late-start for one of the longer circuits.

A typical weekend in Guanajuato – Drew would go off to box in Leon, we'd maybe watch rugby which always disintegrated into a big fight, or baseball, and I'd walk up to one or other of the Presas – with or without company. We could visit Aldo at his uncle's print shop or just sit on the theatre steps and see who turned up. Always there would be alcohol by differing degrees; beer and tequila, rum and coke all readily available, then the homemade Charranda, then mescal and finally Pulque...the cantina Chupilote with its saloon doors, invisible in plain sight, next door to the cathedral, no women allowed.

Like most Pulquerias it had a bathroom-tile facade and an institutional green interior. Pulque is made from maguey like tequila, only not distilled, and has many names; Drool, Babylon, bear soup, vulture soup, white face, moustache broth, chalk and nectar of the gods. It can also be flavoured with tamarind, guava, walnuts, strawberries, beetroot or even celery.

All pulquerias are men-only dives, and without exception have imaginative and evocative names; Pulqueria las duelistas, National Nectar, Ancient Rome, Hen of the Golden Eggs, Firing Line, The worst is nothing, Men without fear. It is a secret and ancient club, protecting its gateway to another world. I never craved it, but there were times when I *needed* it, when I wanted to taste the bitter-sweet sacred cactus milk, just as the gods had been drinking that honey for thousands of years. When I wanted that froth in my moustache, and that alcohol in my veins.

Back at the house, there's a power cut so I sit outside and look down, watching each hill in turn trying to switch itself back on. Like so many other nights the trees still smell of rain and the wall is damp where I sit against it with legs tucked up, just wearing my shorts. Everything smells vaguely dirty, like the half-stale, half-clean smell that the concrete floors take on when they're mopped, the smell I wake up to for two long months as each morning the back door to my bedroom leaks a cascade of water that leaves the whole place flooded, my mattress an island floating to the front door. Outside, the two hundred steps to town, the finite combination of paths becomes a river washing over shit and earth and the odd blade of grass to disappear later miles beneath the houses in the road tunnels that were once purpose-built to divert flood water until the rivers changed course naturally, and the water tamed and trapped above the city's edge in the reservoirs, the blue plaques ten feet above street level an awesome reminder of what aquatic nightmares they once had to put up with, a hint that even here in the mountains we crawled out from the sea. In the wet night my porch's bush has become a tree and the sticky thorns scratch my legs. Scorpions crawl out from behind the light switches. Fernando and the boys are getting ready for a rumble. Tonight it's chains.

TRECE

North of San Miguel de Allende a huge lake provides vistas of women washing clothes and linen on the banks and opens into an area of prairie-like tundra where wide-brim hatted men coax cattle and goats across the vast plains. Rural poverty is abundant, but still the enigma of pro-PRI slogans abound – hand-in-hand with Corona and Coke adverts.

San Miguel is Mexico the way we've come to believe Diego Rivera and Frida Kahlo would have wanted it. There are too many tourists and too many pickpockets, but it takes your breath away. Brightly coloured wooden doors, sleeping guitarists clutching bottles of tequila, and vaqueros riding white horses through town. The expats are smug, and stoically hang on to the San Miguel of ten or twenty years ago in their minds' eye as they go about their daily business of buying foreign newspapers, and drinking coffee. Meanwhile the locals laugh at them behind their backs just as they do the world-over waiting patiently for the day they can draw their knives and slit throats.

There are second-hand book shops here, and boutique antiques the likes of which you would never see in Guanajuato. It doesn't take long to find out where I'd be if I was the Professor. This particular corner of paradise is as much botanical garden as it is hotel café. There are poppies in the bougainvillea, and poppy seeds in the muffins. The fountain has ornamental carp in it. Sitting at the best table, is the man from the bullfight. I know it's him, the Professor. I've never seen a photo, and we've never talked on the phone, but my instincts have been right so far, so why not now? I excitedly introduce myself and outline my quest.

'I'm an old man. I can't help you. I'm sorry you came all this way just to be disappointed.'

That was the end of our first meeting.

I was pissed at the so-called professor. To temper my disillusion, and momentary loss of faith, I decided that a trip to the coast might help. Friends David and Melissa from a large once-Mormon, now seventh-day Adventist family, had a pet iguana which needed releasing back into the wild. Jenny and I volunteered ourselves for the mission.

The Mormons were such a great bunch of people and typical of the broader ex-pat US community in Guanajuato. Men were extraordinarily tall, and lean, with piercing eyes. Women all easy on the eye, young and slim despite delivering eight or nine children a-piece. Nobody had a convincing job history, claiming to sell shoes or swimming pool pumps, making me think that they were all undercover CIA or retired World Bank executives. The clincher for me as a cynic is the dad's professional involvement in, and active recruitment programme for something called NLP, or Neurological Language Programming – brainwashing in anybody's language.

We looked at the map and decided on Playa Azul as the perfect place for us and the reptile to warm our cold blood and rehabilitate a bit. After sixteen hours on a rickety 'chicken' bus, Playa Azul was a hammock-swinging, coconut chopping fun-fest. We drank rum and stayed up late under the stars, listening to the waves on the beach from the hammock that we shared. It was bliss, bringing me and Jenny closer than before. Me made love on the sand, in the surf, in the sea. We jogged and ran, caught fish and ate it cooked in banana leaves with sticky rice bought from the local village. She wore flowers in her hair and never looked sexier, bursting out of her red bikini. I was slim and fit and unashamedly naked most of the time. We released Eric the iguana on day one, at the end of an isthmus where the bushes were thick and we felt he would be safe.

After four glorious love-filled days, Jenny got the bus back to Guanajuato without me – she had to teach and I wanted to head down to Puerto Escondido to be alone and write a bit. I mostly played pool and drank in a bar where we put beer money in an honesty box. There was a freezer with a bottle opener on a long string, and that was it. I was a beach bum author hanging out with surfers who didn't speak to me. To them, I just didn't get it. I was just another uninitiated tourist. Besides, they kept different hours; going to bed early, getting up early. I went to bed late, and got up late. I explored Zipolite – beach of the dead – for a day or two but soon got bored. The Caribbean beckoned and I hitched a little bit further to a place called Playa del Carmen, where I wanted to change some traveller's cheques.

The bank was mercifully freezing. The first air-con I had experienced since leaving the US. Guanajuato didn't have anything this fancy. I joined a long queue and then thought I saw Mike some ways ahead of me, wearing shades and a lurid Hawaiian shirt. He blanched, and turned away. It was only a split-second but I saw it, and knew I wasn't welcome. Why not? Maybe he was here with Dina? I was instantly jealous, and looked around the bank for her in vain. Mike blanked me and walked outside to his jeep, fired up the engine and screeched away in a wheelspin that I'm sure was for my benefit.

CATORCE

As quickly as they had disappeared, Buck and Dina were both back in town and the status quo had been mysteriously resumed. Suddenly everything was back to normal: Dina was waitressing, and Buck was climbing the steps to the university and teaching again, as if nothing had happened.

I'd taken to having breakfast with Jenny, me with nothing better to do, and she in between lessons at the university. Classes started as early as six a.m. especially in summer. The more I learned about her personal life, the more involved I became and I was starting to get jealous. She'd just got back from the VD clinic in Mexico City but I already knew that she was shagging a guy here, while she was 'sick.' Plus she'd had a fling in the capital, and still claimed to be in love with her English boyfriend back home. And, of course, she also loved me. Being her confidante was starting to become tiring.

I was also ill which didn't help. It felt as if someone had cupped their hands to my head and was unceremoniously sucking all the life out of my skull through a straw. Some sort of acute bronchitis that I would suffer from every year for the rest of my life.

Despite still feeling 'chesty', I decided to pull myself together and go to Patzcuaro with Victor, Jenny, Aldo and Dina. We spent Saturday night in Morelia with

English friends of Jenny's and went to a video bar with open pool tables and a live band. Arriving in Patzcuaro on Sunday we found the hippy market and met Victor who had our friend Meryl in tow ('you old dog,' I'm thinking) selling his amber jewellery and other paraphernalia. We had a great day wandering round the market which was full of nardos flowers, baskets, indigenous clothes; and hideous Day of the Dead nik-naks.

For Noche de muertos in Patzcuaro, Dina had elected herself tour-guide. She looked beautiful in tight white jeans, white cotton shirt. Sexy and Mexican. I'd only ever seen her in black biker-cum-Goth clothes. I could sense Jenny tensing up beside me, but she also looked good, wearing short denim shorts and a tight tee-shirt.

Jenny changed into something a little more sombre for the boat ride across to the island of Janitzio. In the evening we used a pipe Jenny bought to get stoned in Victor's hotel room and headed out in canoes towards the island of Janitsio, for the Day of the Dead celebrations. The island is a very steep rock in the middle of a lake. Dina explained that for the local families this was a welcoming back to earth of the deceased family member's spirit. That they would sit and commune with the spirit of that person for the whole night until dawn tomorrow. There was a seemingly endless procession of boats, all carrying lanterns and we could see a procession of lights from the shore of the island cemetery to the grave sites. Once on the island we realised that there were celebrities being followed by film crews and paparazzi as well as hordes of other tourists. Most would go back on the boats but we had already planned to stay the whole night.

'I want to come and live with you.' Jenny was showing a vulnerability I wasn't used to seeing in her, but I still got the message - she was coming. Perhaps it was the shroud of mist hanging over the island cemetery as we sat cuddled up admiring the glow of the myriad candles, that suddenly instilled in her a desire for intimacy.

Hundreds of people came to watch the display by the famous butterfly-boat fishermen and trample through the candle-lit cemetery where local families planted their all-night vigils with offerings of food and possessions for the dead spirits that would return. Slightly stoned as I was, there was a shift in my consciousness which took me a step further away from a young boy in search of a father, and a step closer to a pilgrim on a sacred path.

Due to a decision making crisis induced by, I suspect marijuana, Aldo and I got split up from the girls and Victor. We all ended up staying the night on the island in different parts of the cemetery. Despite searching, it was impossible to find each other by candlelight through a moonless night and mist which rolled in from the lake. The cemetery was void of tourists and as people slept the silence rose into the air as much as the candle light making one of the most powerful scenes. On the way back (it's now fucking cold) our boat got lost in the fog so that the 30 minute journey took an hour but we eventually got back and crashed on the floor of Victor and Meryl's room. We woke up and got stoned again and spent a magic day in the sun before leaving Patzcuaro in one of the world's most tremendous hail storms.

When we got back from Michoacan, Jenny moved in with me from the Bel Air house as promised. The same day both Dobermans jumped the security fence to run free in town with the feral street dogs. Jenny would get up early, at five thirty, to walk to the university and teach at six. I'd either try and get up with her, in an effort to attend my class at seven, or I'd meet her on the steps – me on the way up, she on the way down – coming home from the bar.

QUINCE

Jenny was one of those girls who idolised her parents' marriage, and whilst one side of her sexuality was wild and feckless, she longed to play mother and quite relished her new housewife role, even if we were just play-acting. At this time we met for breakfast almost daily and she'd then come back to the flat after teaching and we'd have time for early lunch and late morning sex before I went to work at the restaurant. If I came home at night I'd find her asleep and we'd cuddle up as happy as any two lovers ever could be.

Dina moved in more by osmosis. After one of our parties where she and several other people had slept on the floor, she stayed intermittently for a week. She was just there. Quietly working on whatever it was she was working on, and doing long shifts at Chicago's.

Jenny was quite snobby about some things, one of which was going to the doctor. She would rather travel all the way to Mexico City to go to a 'good' doctor. The local doctor – that most of the expats went to – was a bit of a drunkard and made her feel uncomfortable. He'd been in Mexico for almost thirty years, and was quite a character, often seen after hours in the bars in his wheelchair. In an emergency, though, Mexico City might as well have been on the other side of the moon. I wasn't always privy to Jenn's personal movements so it came as no surprise that she'd been visiting the doc without me knowing. What did come as a surprise, was *why* she'd been going to see him.

Jenny's period was late; she had allowed maybe fifty per cent of her emotions to prepare for pregnancy and parenthood with me, but the overwhelming sensation was now one of relief.

Through the open door, Guanajuato and its ring of green hills were getting ready for another Mexican sunset. I was finding my satori, right here in paradise. Humming birds and naked girls had become almost commonplace. The smell of sex, mingling with willow sap and the damp dust. I thought of the Professor's sexually-explicit gift to me, a signed copy of his own Mexican novel; "Kissing their fuck, am I?" the heroine asked as she added her mouth to the friends' intimate congress. It was a handicapped threesome, her crippled hand fumbling here and there.

Dina quickly became naked as if it was the most natural thing in the world, which it was of course, and I marvelled at her smooth skin and perfect curves as she leant over me.

'How did you get such a big dick, Henry?'

She had a relatively hairy, boxlike bush which, like her was a little bit aggressive – it knew what it wanted and how to get it.

We kissed and then started to make love on the big cushions in the corner of the room. I felt rather than watched Jenny wake up, flinch, and go back into the bedroom. I pumped Dina a few more times, but stood up without coming and went to see Jenny.

I walked across the cold concrete floor naked with my erection bouncing along nicely in front of me. Jenny was on top of the sheet, and just waking up. I grabbed one of her boobs and squeezed it. Before she had time to complain I kissed her hard on the mouth and moved to enter her from behind. She winced.

'Maybe later,' she smiled, 'why don't you finish what you started?'

It was a good way of disarming me, diffusing the situation. She put a record on – *Love's in need of love today*. On my way back to Dina, I grabbed a bottle of tequila and some cut limes. I found her outside, fingering herself in the hammock.

'Did you fuck her?' Dina asked.

'No.' I lied.

I kissed her pussy while she was still in the hammock. She sat on a rock and sucked me off for a bit before penetration was resumed, me on my knees in the dirt, hard as a hammer watching hummingbirds in the cacti flowers, laughing, gently biting her neck as I came loudly, a split second after she did.

DIECISÉIS

The bloody memory of Montezuma's worst defeat was etched into Tezcatlipoca's consciousness.

As the morning mist rolled habitually across the lake's surface it hinted at a scale of carnage only wholly apparent once the morning sun had come up one hour later. A spear here, a helmet there. Next a bare torso, its severed head bobbing awkwardly some metres away.

The Lord of the Smoking Mirror had walked these gangplanks, so gallantly and patriotically defended, many times since that day. Asleep, awake. In this world, and the next. It didn't matter which and didn't change the outcome, the balance of power that shifted that day forcing the occult to bury itself deeper while the world began its ill-fated love affair with Christianity. Planks awash with blood. The army – his army – that had been cut down as the Spanish horses galloped through the water (charging the flash; the flash of the sun on the flat water, its reflection on their armour and the flash of their own canons) laid six deep in some places.

Conquistador casualties had only been high at the beginning of the battle until Cortes himself had appeared and confused some who'd thought he was a god. Thus the acolytes were torn apart for their divided loyalties and Tezcatlipoca himself would gladly have smote the emperor had it been wise to but the calendar wheel had already foretold what path the stars and planets would take and who was he (even he) to question.

Women had come in canoes to silently lay wreaths while others tossed blooms into the waters of Xochimilco. Multicoloured petals mingled with the blue blood and white pelicans with bright orange bills came to paddle quietly and fish. Even the giant seabirds, the cormorants and albatrosses, found carrion (flesh) on which to feast.

Fish also began to pick clean the bones and rats brave enough to swim found food for themselves for weeks.

The vultures of that day still occupied Tezcatlipoca's imagination. Silhouettes like black paper aeroplanes circling in their thousands. It was impossible nowadays to see such carnage and receive so many new souls. First he would retrieve the mask and recruit Henry. Then he would begin all over again.

Guanajuato's hills strewn with secret caves and steep, shady overhangs were now embroidered with ornate and archaeologically significant art thanks to him. These were talismanic drawings that his Excellency the giver of life and death had spent the whole night drawing. No one could hex him again here. Not now.

He began to feel invincible and needed a woman, several women in fact.

TERCERA PARTE

DIECISIETE

Colonel Tim McClure, ex-United States Army turned United States Army Military Police investigator, is convinced that he is getting too old to be chasing renegade soldiers. His long limbs are stiff from driving, his stomach is telling him it's time for supper and his eyes are telling him it's bed time. Matt Harroldson, his young sidekick, however, is ambitious and chivvies him along. Harroldson has a theory. But for all McClure cares Buck Buchanan can keep his mouth shut and live out the rest of his days in rural Mexico. Good for him. The guy is a hero for God's sake. McClure can't decide who he wants to go to hell in a handcart more; Buck Buchanan or the garrulous Harroldson?

In the course of Harroldson's background research, continues the upstart over-enthusiastically, one of his questions to establish whether there was, in fact, a motive for running to Mexico has been to ask did Buck ever mention it? Two of Buck's Vietnam contemporaries remembered some sort of prize possession which Buck had unearthed in a Saigon market towards the end of the war. Apparently, the day he found it Buck had let slip that he thought it was a valuable and pre-Columbian Mexican artefact, and that when this was all over he would go and check it out. But that was the one and only reference and neither roommate had ever seen the object. Hence the young detective harboured romantic notions that this was not only a man-hunt but also a treasure-hunt. A day spent interviewing a bunch of US expat, ex-frat kids who knew nothing, was a day on the road to Tim McClure's imminent retirement wasted.

The MP's had had a tip off that Buck liked to smoke pot (who didn't?), and word on the street was that if you wanted to buy it in Guanajuato, this would be the place to come to. The witch house.

Consequently, Casa de las Brujas had become a hive of activity. The MP's had got a whiff of Buck's trail, yes, but as was becoming all-too-apparent to them they were barking up the wrong tree. *If* Buck smokes dope and *if* he occasionally buys grass from these guys, he would never hang out at this house. *If* he's hiding in Guanajuato. If he's not at home getting high, then he might be out having a beer or two, but these stoners never leave the house and wouldn't know that about him. In fact the dope-heads are adamant that they have never even heard of anyone in Guanajuato by that name.

It was bent over his third helping of tacos at Taco Inn in Guanajuato that Harroldson had persuaded McClure to visit Leon first so that they could go and check out the upcoming bullfight.

'It can't be all work and no play, surely?'

For once the old colonel couldn't agree more, and he allowed himself a brief Mexican-retirement-fantasy of his own. One where the Tex-Mex of his North American life was also available south of the border; he wondered if his six-foot three frame would ever again be filled with food, and flirted (at least mentally) with the idea of drinking alcohol. Getting gloriously drunk on beer and tequila, and messing around with two of the girls they'd met at the Witch House earlier.

One glance at Harroldson confirmed that he'd

never known the pleasures of women of the night; the thrill of a threesome whether he'd earned it – or paid for it – or not. In the same fantasy, the wife did not come to Mexico straight away after his retirement, preferring instead to stay behind in the States while the second and third-born children finished university. Because it was the right thing to do.

Harroldson was busy trying to pay; he was tired and wanted to go back to the hotel.

McClure tried to remember the names of the two girls. Dina and Jenny? Neither of them had heard of anyone called Buck but they *had* made him (McClure) think about his groin. Jenny with her upper-middle class English accent, and naturally large boobs. Dina with her slutty Amer-exican slang and a great ass, like a young boy's. He could hear the sound of the waves lapping at the beach from his hammock. Parrots and hummingbirds flying amongst the flowers, and wasn't that a pelican? And the stars…how could he ever describe the beauty of the Mexican night sky?

Harroldson would never understand that McClure had no agenda to snag Buck in a trap and bring him home to be tormented by senior-ranking officials in a tedious war crimes tribunal. McClure had also seen action and knew what it meant to be the one who stopped the horror – the whistleblower. So Buck was a hero. Harroldson could play his game, but they would always be one or two steps behind.

Retirement would mean an end to such conundrums. It would bring peace. If he and Mrs McClure had been all-but estranged for the past few years it was what they both knew and had become comfortable with. They stayed together for the kids but also because they both believed in the sanctity of their wedding vows. Fuck it; maybe he would have that drink. Maybe he would find

Buck at the bull fight and not even tell Harroldson? They could sit and have drinks together, maybe go wild, go whoring!

The bill came to interrupt his daydreaming, and it was time to go back to the hotel. What was it one of the girls had said at the Witch House? 'No se puede vivir sin amar?' You can't live without love. He took it to mean that life was too short not to love, to not enjoy it. And she was right. His whole life he'd lived by the rules – knowing the right path, and walking it. Straight down the line, all the way. Wasn't there one last chance for him to ride into town on his horse and shoot it up a little bit? Mexico made him feel like a lone gunslinger, and he longed to dump his sidekick. Let's see what mañana would bring.

Not a day went by that he didn't remember the exact time and place his marriage had started to deteriorate. June 30th 1988, in Puerto Vallarta. Noreen aka Mrs McClure had begged him not to overreact, not to go down there but he was damned if he was going to stand by and do nothing while his son was in trouble the wrong side of the border. What Noreen didn't know, and would never know was exactly how Colonel McClure had remedied the situation. But it didn't matter, she knew her husband well enough to know that he'd hurt someone, and that was enough; he was forever branded a Neanderthal. Ironic really, as he knew she was proud of his military career.

DIECIOCHO

Playa del Carmen, Cancun

A single prop Piper Aztec, sole charter paid in cash, took off from the island of Cozumel and after only twenty minutes in the air landed on a beach not far from Playa del Carmen – then a collection of bamboo and grass beach huts and one or two café-bars, not the resort it is now. The pilot was just doing his job. When he got paid in advance like this, he didn't ask too many questions. The cargo's journey had started in Thailand, and consisted of bulk clothing and curios headed for a gift shop somewhere in Mexico. That's all he knew and all he cared to know.

Meeting the plane were a man and woman team, high on coke and happy as pigs in shit as they smoked dope and loaded the bundles of shoes, sarongs, teeshirts and jewellery into the back of their Jeep. Back at the house, just a few clicks along the sand – a luxury cabaña which had enough trees surrounding it to ensure privacy – the square bundles were cut open and dissected and packets of cocaine which had gone undetected were counted and weighed. The buyer arrived by boat after a pre-arranged pattern of lights gave him the 'all clear.' Weighing and paying took two hours which meant that the buyer and his team still left under cover of darkness.

Jose Cuervo and Coke saw the happy couple

through – exhausted – to the dawn; a sunrise swim, sex on the beach and a breakfast of pancakes with pineapple and mango smoothies.

In the bank wearing a Hawaiian shirt and flip-flops, carrying $50, 000 cash in a string bag more used to bringing oranges home from the shops or taking a towel and a book to the beach, Mike waited nervously. In Aviators. The night before was taking its toll on his nerves. He was wiring the money to the Cayman Islands. He'd done it before, it would all be over in half an hour. From the corner of his eye, he saw, but didn't want to see, someone he knew very well.

Transaction completed he left the air-conditioned bank and started to sweat as soon as he hit the street and headed for the Jeep, which was parked opposite. He waited for a gap in the traffic and felt that his shirt was sticking to his back before he even got into the driver's seat. Whenever he sniffed or swallowed, he could taste cocaine and he involuntarily clenched his teeth together. His nerves were shot and he knew he was still incapable of getting the sleep his body craved. He lit a Marlboro red with the car cigarette lighter, flicked on the radio and pulled out.

'Fuck,' he was thinking. 'What in hell's name is that fucking bastard doing in Playa del Carmen? Shit.'

Mike pulled over to buy a cold Coke from the carwash guys at the next lights. There was hardly any traffic, which would have made it impossible for anyone to tail him unnoticed. He let the Mexicans do the front windshield while he surreptitiously checked and double-checked the street.

At the green light he swung the Jeep back into the road and drove fast, straight for the beach. He left the blacktop and tore along a strip of wet sand at the surf line. White foam kicked up from behind the wide off-road tyres like two jets behind a speed boat. He was pulling away from the cabin, but intended to get back there in a large loop. There was nothing untoward about the scene he witnessed flashing past him. A woman he knew who always walked her dog at this time; the dog was barking at him. A family setting up a picnic. A couple lying on their backs in swimming trunks and bikini. Surfers paddling towards the next wave. He stopped abruptly and his Aviators fell half-way off his face.

Mike pushed the shades back up to the bridge of his nose and he lit another cigarette. Fuck. Dina! His persecution complex had allowed him to leave her alone in the cabaña, and he now thought she might be in danger.

Buck found Dina by the pool, where she was wearing only white shorts and sunglasses. The local beach radio station was pumping out classic rock hits through the open French windows. She acknowledged his presence with a smile and shouted, 'Would you like a drink? Or a swim?'

She jumped into the pool holding her beer, sunglasses on, with a cigarette in her mouth. 'Or a fuck?' she coughed as she came up.

They both laughed. After all they used to be lovers.

Buck went inside and bought two more cold beers from the refrigerator, and turned down the radio slightly; hoping that she wouldn't notice and think that he was old. He tried to put out of his mind the shape of Dina's bush which clearly showed through her wet shorts.

'I saw Mike in the bank. What are you guys up to?' He put a wedge of lime in the top of her Corona and handed it over.

'Aww, you turned the music down, man! Shit. Thanks for the beer.' She squeezed the lime into the neck of the bottle and took a swig, 'we're on vacation. Well, that plus picking up supplies for the shop.'

She made straight for the house to turn the volume back up but he caught her arm and stopped her.

'This is some serious shit, Dina, if I think you guys are doing what I think you're doing.'

'And what would that be, Buck?' She snapped, accusing him of all the bad shit he'd ever done in his life with one quick look. She had very little patience for this real-world trouble stuff and he knew it. She took off her wet shorts and picked up the sarong she'd been lying on, letting him see her naked. She kissed him full on the lips, before wrapping herself.

'If only life was as simple as you think it is.' He said and shook his head. Memories of a younger Buck and an even younger Dina were suppressed.

Just then the gunning of an engine told them that Mike was back and Buck's heckles were instantly raised. He went straight out to the car and punched Mike full in the face. Mike made a brief attempt to get up and retaliate but Buck hit him hard in the ribs. Mike was broken.

'You think I'm fucking stupid? You dumb fuck! You think you can use my wife's business to bring drugs into the country? You'd better think of a good reason why I shouldn't kill you!'

Mike's mind was racing. How in hell had Buck not only figured out what he was up to, but also figured out the time and the place? No one knew that shit, not even Dina. He was a dead man, he knew. A has-been musician from the Guanajuato State Orchestra, washed up on the beach after a late-night mugging. It happened all the time. He could see his bloated white corpse with tiny red crabs running in and out of his nose and mouth, the long black hair and the goatee inanimate in the surf against his white skin. Only later would it come out that he was once famous in the States. That he had debts as a result of a drug problem and a bad recording deal. Ironically, he thought to himself before the pain of his broken nose and bruised ribs filtered through to his nervous system, a couple more of these trips and he'd be home free in terms of what he owed. He felt a new pain as Buck's hands tightened around his neck, and the world grew suddenly dark.

'BUCK. Buck' It was Dina, shouting at first, then almost whispering to him now. 'Buck, I can think of a good reason. Come on, let's go for a walk. Ven aca, mi amor.' Her words had the desired soothing effect. Buck released his grip. She glanced sideways at Mike and he took his queue to go inside and clean up, as soon as he'd fully regained consciousness.

Dina took Buck's arm and gave him another beer. She lit a joint and they walked towards the beach. Dina somehow always managed to look the part: A baseball cap and a man's oversized tee-shirt were perfect for sundowners on the beach. Yet it was effortless, and you wouldn't say she was tarty – unless you knew her, that is.

Buck still had a thousand-yard stare etched into his face, but at least he was back. Sunset had made the sea calm and flat as it often does and Buck's forehead glowed orange as he perched on top of a dune. Dina was lying flat on her back facing the other way, inland. He and Dina had been sitting and talking for a while. Dina had used persuasion and pragmatism to convince him that killing Mike really wasn't a viable option. Firstly, the current set-up was netting $50, 000 dollars every three months; secondly, Buck wasn't a soldier any more, he couldn't just go around killing people; and thirdly, they were friends. In love, and in business, together.

It wasn't an award-winning speech but Buck found it quite cute. Dina's Mexican-English accent and her occasional loss for words where she'd used the Spanish reminded him of his wife, Carmen, when he had first met her and she'd also got lost or tripped up and frustrated without the word she thought was there – on the tip of her tongue – but wasn't. His little voice was still telling him that Mike was no good, that he'd fucked up and had to be dealt with, but he was ignoring it. His hunch had been correct. The surveillance had been perfect. All that was left to complete the mission was to kill Mike. Tie up the loose ends. Dina would never understand, and neither would Carmen. He made to get up and leave but Dina stopped him.

'Let's make love, Buck. One last time. No one need ever know?' He turned to look at her, and in her eyes he saw something of the little girl trying to take on the whole universe who had first seduced him almost two years earlier. Saving the whole world one white man at a time. She smiled and kissed him, and started to unbuckle his belt.

DIECINUEVE

Dina was a muralist in the purest sense of the word. For her, each mural was a truly spiritual event, a journey to a broader understanding of the cosmos. She bared her soul in such a sensual expression of life that it often spilled over into the house she was working in. She would feel compelled to make love to whoever was commissioning the painting; male or female. Each painting was an outward projection of her inner self. In life she hid very little; in her art she hid nothing at all. Swirling vaginas were not simply the essence of woman, they were *her* essence, *her* lust for life and *her* sex. The colours were vivid and resplendent yet earthy as per the finest traditions and her themes paired motorbikes and heavy metal guitars, with pastoral scenes of washing clothes and sowing seeds.

Buck's commission came about by accident. It was Carmen who mentioned it.

'Mi amor. I think we should decorate our little niño's room, don't you?'

'Yes, of course. What did you have in mind?'

'A mural. A good old-fashioned Mexican mural. After all this *is* the town where Diego Rivera was born, and I want our baby girl to be blessed by the old gods as well as the new one.'

'I agree. It's a great idea, but I'm not that good at painting. I'll give it my best shot.'

'I know you will, querido. But I was thinking maybe a Mexican could do it, you know? I hear there's a young girl in town and she's very talented. You're not offended, mi vida?'

'Offended? No. Relieved, maybe.' He laughed and pulled his wife closer as they stood in the soon-to-be nursery room.

Buck cast his mind back to a time before Dina, and Carmen and Mexico. He wasn't generally much given to reflection, but as he lay on the beach with the setting sun, he thought about his life and wondered what the future held for him and his small family? Had he done enough to set up his wife and son, should anything happen to him? Was he a good father and husband? He thought about his own parents, who had risked everything to sail to the States from war-torn Europe. A father who had held the world in the palm of his hand but had slipped inexorably (after the death of his wife) into the cynical clutches of alcoholism. Buck had had a hard life. Losing his parents and his first love, all before he even went to war. Vietnam had been every bit as hellish as he'd expected. Had he had a good war? It didn't do to dwell on that shit. The best thing to come out of Saigon was the jade funeral mask which he had had valued at $1, 000, 000 USD, and which never left his side, day or night. Maybe it was time to sell it? He suspected that it wouldn't be much longer before the authorities stateside redoubled their efforts to find him.

Dina was young when he first bumped into her, a friendly seventeen year-old. A sexy teenager who impressed Buck with her force of personality, and never-say-die attitude. She knew what she wanted and for several glorious weeks, he had been it. He found a second-hand bike, a Norton, and they would ride off into the hills to explore the presas and abandoned mines. One ruined village had a beautiful church in it and they would picnic there, and fuck there. One day Dina found a trap door which led to steps and a tunnel system that ended up underneath one of the old silver mines. It had remained their secret. Dina was convinced that this was how the famous Isabelle's husband had smuggled his wealth out of the mine, but for Buck the electric lights told him another story; namely that the smugglers' route was either still in use, or had been until very recently.

Nogales is a big border town like Tijuana, with all the excitement and associated problems. For the first five years of Dina's life, it was fine. Then her mother fled, and left her daughter at the mercy of an abusive father. During the next twelve years Dina saw things, and was made to do things that no child should ever endure. Consequently she tied her tubes at fifteen (the soonest she could persuade the doctors to do the operation), determined never to bring another person into such a cruel world, and certainly not a child fathered by her own father or a bastard by his cronies. He was a useless, two-bit criminal, her father. A drunkard, gang member, pornographer. Tough as she was, she was frightened for her life whenever she considered exacting retribution, or revenge, or more specifically violent revenge. What would they do if she wielded a knife or a gun? Laugh at her? Shoot her up a bit? Cut her tits off? She was just another cunt to them.

She found the courage to run and spent a year hitching and riding in buses all over Mexico. She only stopped being scared and started to feel a little safer when she stumbled upon Guanajuato in the midst of the Sierra Madre. A beautiful jewel of a town – nestled in between mountains – where somebody can hide, and start over. It was a university town, and she would be born-again, reinventing herself as a bohemian Goth biker. She would paint. She would become an artist.

Buck saw a mural Dina was doing on the

pavement in crayon, and asked if she could come to the house and decorate his study. It was a dangerous affair. He was three times older than her, and the wife (pregnant at the time) was often in the main house while Dina painted the walls and roof of his folly-cum-study at the bottom of the garden, in torn denim dungarees.

VEINTE

If Henry was feeling Diego Rivera's nudes – the girl sweeping up the Calla lilies in her arms and pulling them towards her breast; the bather at the lake with boobs dangling; the sensuous 'Mujer de rodillas con girasoles' and the beautiful 'Nieves desnuda de rodillas sobre un petate' – Jenny was feeling Frida Kahlo. To wear her pain, the physical pain left by the tram wreck and the emotional pain of trying to be a beautiful woman in other people's eyes, so publicly. It was an artistic crusade that spoke to her even before she'd set foot inside the Coyoacan house but afterwards she felt as if her soul had been touched by a friend. It was an emotion, a spiritual awakening, unlike anything she'd experienced before. She went back to Guanajuato with a deep yearning to share what she'd seen and felt. Henry and Dina just happened to be in the firing line.

The doctor at the genito-urinary disease clinic had been quite cute and if her lips hadn't been quite so sensitive and swollen still, she'd probably have gone for it. Gonorrhea and vaginal thrush. Have you had unprotected sex recently? Define recently. He gave her antibiotic tablets and a cortisone cream plus a little bit of relationship counselling. It was before the days of mandatory AIDS testing but he nevertheless asked her if she knew her status. She agreed to a test and then waited for twenty anxious minute before he called her back in to look at the results. He opened it in front of her and they both noted the single control line showing that it was negative. Jenny's heart started to beat faster. She gave him her best smile and wished they would meet again. She would come back soon, of course.

Jenny turned her back on the cool of the house and embraced the furnace of outside at mid-day with an open heart and a pair of Ray Bans. Her denim hot pants and cropped grey Gap tee-shirt did justice to her figure. She was feeling frisky and ready to leave the villa with all its old people overtones and underlying strictness. It had served her well on arrival, an island of luxury away from Guanajuato's day-to-day chaos but now she was ready for something else. Jenny didn't shut the door, consciously allowing the Dobermans who had both tried to rape her, to escape and run riot in town until either the city dogcatcher or the head gardener captured them and hopefully euthanased them. She tried to remember where Henry's flat was and how to get there in a taxi, she was not going to traipse across town in this heat with her bags to get there; that was Henry's style, but not hers. She had been thinking about Henry for several days, or was it weeks, now? Why did he never kiss her, reach for her, take her? They'd been alone many times and even slept together in the same bed, on the bus, and in a hammock by the sea. The furthest he'd taken it was an arm briefly across her shoulders. It was her horny time of the month and nothing was going to stop her being Henry's; he who had inadvertently touched all of the wrong (meaning right) buttons.

Patrick had just back from Central America – tall, tanned, relaxed – he had a big laugh and big hands. Patrick and his entourage were just leaving Chicago's when Jenny ran up the steps to ask Buck or Dave or any of the regulars how to get to Henry's hill. He blocked her path with a muscular forearm and a large, confident grin, 'Where are *you* going in such a hurry? I thought we had a drinks' appointment.'

'Ummm,' Jenny's mind was racing and she thought for a split-second that she might fight the inevitability of him getting in her knickers, but more out of habit than anything else she played along. 'Remind me, dear, when and where were we supposed to meet again?'

'That little place next door, with the funny painted hands on the wall.'

'Give me five minutes,' Jenny laughed and continued running up the steps.

Patrick's friends scoffed and rolled their eyes, obviously having seen this kind of blatant flirting before.

Later, as Jenny took off her bra and let Patrick glimpse and grab her breasts for the first time she just wanted to be held, she wasn't in the mood for a vulva-bashing session and was with Patrick simply because he was good looking and it was expected of her, well of both of them in fact. But Patrick was a rugby jock and he wasn't about to be gentle with Jenny, the big-breasted Jewish hottie who'd fallen for his lady-killing charm, he'd had a few drinks and was in the mood to bring it on – he'd make her come five times and see if he could make her ejaculate – he wanted to lift her up and throw her around the room the whole night.

She wanted him to stick it in and finish quickly, just to feel a man between her legs would be enough, to feel his weight on top of her. But Patrick obviously had other ideas and was more into a one-night-stand porn-epic session that would have broken a lesser experienced lover. Jenny moaned in pain as he thrust into her too hard and hit her womb with his dick, instantly regretting her gamble.

'I think you're fucking fit,' he said into her ear as

he grabbed a handful of her thick hair and pulled her head back, expecting her to be impressed. She pushed against his chest with both hands and groaned in disagreement but he was spurred on, quickly misinterpreting her abeyance as a green light for more violence. Jenny thought quickly and said, 'Let me go on top,' even though she knew the angle would hurt her again. She flicked her hips and brought him to the edge of coming much more quickly than he'd wanted.

'Give it to me big boy,' she screamed in faux excitement and sped up another notch. Patrick was confused and she slid off him, worried that he was going to change positions and drill her from behind or carry her into the shower, she took the condom off and started going down on him, kneeling on the floor at the foot of the bed as she sucked his dick and scratched his hairy chest with her long nails.

'What the fuck?' Before he could complain she was kneading his balls and expertly jerking the foreskin over the bell-end until he came involuntarily. 'What was that all about? Is it your period?'

Jenny felt dirty and was not sure whether or not this stranger was going to hit her for denying him, so she dressed quickly and gave him practiced eyes. 'I'm sorry, it's just that I have a boyfriend…and yes I'm due. Very hormonal… Maybe next time?' She left the hotel room and was disappointed to find it was still daylight outside, all she wanted was to be invisible in the darkness, to slip unseen through the shadows and find Henry.

When she finally got to the house it was dark and Jenny, now tired, let herself in through the open door. One or two tea lights cut through the gloom and the flat smelled of incense. She gently pushed the bedroom door and closing it behind her got undressed and lay down next to the prone body under the covers. There was something familiar about the sweet smell and the soft skin, but in the darkness it was not easy to tell who the body belonged to. Her hands found hair and breasts and welcoming lips that brushed her eyelids and forehead and she was finally embraced and held with the security that had been so absent earlier.

'Quien es? Jenny, eres tú?'

'Sí.'

'Te estaba esperando – I was waiting for you.'

'En sério?'

'Sí. De vez en cuando yo veo al futuro.'

'Where's Henry?'

'He's still at work. Or out drinking…he's probably in the bars looking for us.' Dina smiled in the darkness and kissed Jenny on the forehead. Dina's hands brushed against Jenny's breasts and rested on her hips. Jenny sank deeper into her reverie taking refuge in the caresses.

'Estás bien? Are you ok?' Dina asked.

'Yes, I am now.'

'Something happened?'

'I fucked up and got hurt, I'll be ok.'

'A man?'

'Yes.'

'Do you want a drink? I'm dying for a smoke. We could go down the hill into town if you like?'

'No, let's wait here.'

VEINTIUNO

In the sacristy I saw lying about three empty cases, but the silver crucifixes and chalices they once contained had been carried off by Mexican thieves. The man in charge of the building showed me three immense drawers full of gold- and silver-embroidered silken robes of exquisite fineness and great variety.

There were at least several dozens of them. The altar-piece was arranged and painted very tastefully in red and gold. Several oil paintings were hanging in the church, but so darkened by the hand of time that it was impossible to make out whether they were of any artistic merit. Wonderful men those early missionaries, who brought such valuables into this wilderness, over hundreds and thousands of miles, on the backs of mules or Indians. It was rather anomalous to see the poor, naked Indians outside the door, for whose benefit all this had been done. A woman was sweeping away the dirt from the swarms of bats that nested in the ceiling.

I descended through magnificent groves of cedar-trees to Pueblo Nuevo, making my camp on top of a hill, from which I overlooked the little settlement and the valley in which it nestles. As every house is surrounded by its little garden of orange-trees, aguacates, and guayahas, the landscape presented a mass of verdure of different shades, the ugly, often dilapidated houses being almost lost in the green. Lemons grow wild, and therefore there is no sale for them. Lemon juice mixed with milk is in many parts of Mexico considered a remedy for dysentery.

A young priest, who exercised a supreme but judicious

authority in this secluded spot, treated me with much consideration. He took an honest pride in the development of his little village, and showed me its sights, first the church, which he was embellishing in many ways, and then the spring which supplied the place with water, and where the women gathered to wash their clothes and gossip. We met many graceful figures carrying jars on their shoulders, as in ancient times.

With a certain hubris I began to settle into my role as drunken master.

I had two fingers deep inside Jenny. She moaned and habitually hid her one slightly deformed hand under the pillow. She was wet and we kissed, deep passionate kisses, I pulled off her tee shirt and tore off her panties with my teeth, deliberately ripping them.

'Hen…'

'Don't worry, I'll buy you a new pair,' I grinned. I went to piss.

It was dawn, the first dirty rays of light entering the bedroom where our makeshift curtain didn't quite reach. Dina had fallen asleep on the cushions by the fire in the other room.

Jenny lay prone on the bed with her legs apart and pelvis thrust towards me when I got back. I grabbed her heavy breasts and kneaded them before gently kissing both nipples, one at a time. I caressed her head of curls with both hands and let my erection fall into her mouth where she obligingly sucked twice, salivated and opened her Epiglottis. I pulled away before coming to lie down between her legs and start kissing her there.

Jenny's future hinged on her getting a first from Cambridge. She may have been having the time of her life in Mexico but already the fact that she'd missed her A level grades (with AABB, instead of a predicted AAAB) to study Medicine or Law at Oxford was a serious embarrassment.

The Cambridge post-grad expats were under a lot of pressure to get good grades throughout their programme.

One day after the state taxi drivers' strike was Saint Agnes' day. There were union strikes, national holidays and Catholic holidays for a whole week. Then it was Cervantino. Guanajuato was flooded with an influx of thousands, the streets and bars were full, the hotels were full. There were fireworks day and night. Some people came for the art galleries and the plays – all the better known plazas had been converted into open-air theatres and cinemas but for the town itself it would be a two-week long fiesta.

I skipped down the steps in my own world somewhat. Kids threw Chinese firecrackers at me from their roofs as I ran down past them but I was unfazed. Starbursts of other fireworks filled the tiny crack of night sky high above the callejon. At the foot of the alley in town I ran smack into a life-size effigy of Sancho Panza. I looked up and found Don Quijote dangling above the sea of heads fifty yards further into the square. My little sugarcoated peanut and torta stand haven had been invaded. I was trying to get to Rocinantes and should have turned left on the shortcut but ran past it.

A group of kids dressed as skeletons ran against the flow of the crowd throwing flour and eggs at each other.

I saw the doctor's wheelchair disappearing between El Truco and Mary Magdalane church and ducked out of the crowd to try and get to the bar faster through the jardín. After two Dos Equis oscura and two tequila shots…

VEINTIDÓS

Recently I walked home past the Witch House and saw two black, SUV-type vehicles which looked out of place. They're new and nobody here has that kind of money, or at least if they do, it's not spent on anything so ostentatious.

Pablo, my soon-to-be ex-landlord, drove past in his old VW Beetle which is German, not Brazilian or Argentinean or – heaven forbid – Mexican. He explained that he couldn't give me a lift, indicating with a wave of his hand that the whole car was piled high with nappies for his niece. That's ok, I tell him, because I prefer walking and don't want a lift. I rarely see his niece, but her constant wailing is very much part of life in the crazy courtyard at his house, which is just next door to mine. Maybe she has Downs' syndrome or is mentally ill. I struggle with the idea that she is trapped and hidden away in this heat.

*****

Dave Erf, Chicago's' proprietor, wearing an oversized white polo shirt wobbles over to our table where I'm tucking into a pre-shift pizza with Buck and trying to catch up on my diary. We're sitting by the window watching the second half of *The Empire Strikes Back* which is on TV. The sun's low rays indicate the onset of night. Buck is already drunk.

Mr. Erf hasn't been in our lives for very long. He just turned up one day and started recruiting. Offering free food, free booze, wages and tips, it was impossible to say no to him.

'I've been in books before,' Buck tells me, with a nod towards my diary.

'None that I've read,' I think to myself. The information doesn't surprise me, though.

Dave's grey slacks, worn chest high over his paunch, expose bright yellow socks. Ice clinks as vodka and fresh orange sloshes around in his glass. His reading glasses, hung from a chain round his neck, sway from side to side. Sweat beads glisten on his bald head defying any attempt to mop them up with a folded handkerchief.

'You know, Henny. I just like to fuck. Back in the 70's my friends used to have this joke. They'd line up a great fat line of pure Colombian cocaine, place a bottle of Jack Daniel's on one side, with a Blue-label Smirnoff next to it and a doughnut on the other side. I used to be able to say cocaine, no; vodka, no; whisky, no; but I could never say no to the doughnut!

Every night they'd be high on coke or booze in the little room out back, but I tell ya, my drug was always sex. While they were all too fucked up to do anything, I'd be upstairs fucking my brains out, and I'd go home sober. Or just go home to the wife. He heehe.' As he talks and drinks I watch the perspiration and Screwdriver juice trapped in his greying stubble and wait for him to either lick it off or wipe it up. His eyes sparkle as he remembers pussy-past and ingests the day's first drink.

This is where I first met Dina, Chicago's. Before she became a waitress she would come in and read a book. She had the bookish student thing down pat; looking sexy with her hair tied up, wearing a man's shirt with round-rimmed John Lennon glasses. Little did I know that that's what she did best; appearing as her next prey's most desired woman. She'd somehow gleaned that I liked literature and as I was next on the hit-list, she simply projected what I would want in a Mexican chick. She was an accomplished chameleon.

I'd just taken my usual seat and started to think about writing. In the kitchen Toni was already preparing my staff pizza, a large peperoni, which was mouthwateringly good. I salivated thinking about it and sipped my Diet Coke. I didn't want to take the best window seat in case a paying customer came in so I was tucked away in the corner near Dave's bedroom where I couldn't even see the TV. Dina hadn't yet started to work with us and I didn't know her by name but I'd seen her around. For the past three days she had been in the restaurant alone; just reading. She sat in the centre of the room which says a lot about a person I think. I mean most people when faced with a near-empty restaurant would not choose to sit where everybody else could see them but it didn't seem to bother her. She had her black curly hair pulled back and up in a kind of bun. The look was cute but I was not immediately turned on by her, I was not buying it. Not buying it yet, that is. This stage was all part of a plan. Her plan. Eventually – as she already knew – I would buckle under the pressure and ask her what she was reading.

'Hi, what are you reading?'

'Dostoyevsky.' It was so over the top that I had to hold back a smirk.

'My god, that is heavy going.'

'Yeah it's hard work but I love it.' She took off her glasses and closed the book. 'Can I get a menu?'

'Sure, here you go. Where are you from? Your accent is very American.'

'Nogales, near the border.'

'Is it...'

'A shithole? Yeah, it's a shithole. Why do you think I came to University here? Guanajuato's beautiful.' She was all business; short, quick answers.

'Yes, I love Guanajauato.' Toni came out of the kitchen with my pizza. With a toothless grin and a nod of the head he silently asked where he should put it? 'Thanks Toni, just put it over there.' Then to Dina, 'Would you like to sit with me and share my pizza? It's big enough.' I lied, I always ate a whole one to myself.

We sat together and ate pizza. Two bites in she ordered more jalapeños with Toni in Spanish. When she'd finished her half she asked if she could excuse herself, there was somewhere she had to be. We both stood up and then did the customary cheek-kiss thing. For the shortest second I smelled her hair and scent. I was left hungry and confused. Love at first sight it was not. Not quite.

Two days later when I turned up to start my next shift I was surprised to find Dina wearing an apron and white uniform polo shirt.

'Hi Henny, this is Dina,' said Dave grinning broadly and mouthing 'fuckee fuckee?' behind her back putting his index finger into the other hand's fist repeatedly.

I would have preferred to work with my friend Aldo but I knew he'd already gone to Leon to prepare for the big regional bullfighting festival.

'Hola Henry, cómo estás?' Dina seemed to be far too intimate with Dave, and the body language worried me. Was he fucking her already? Why was I so jealous?

In the kitchen she was on good terms with Toni and the team. Her cold demeanour from two days ago had all-but vanished and she was starting to change tactics. The glasses had gone and the hair was down. Her legs and behind looked good in the apron. She kept catching my attention and silently maintaining eye contact until I felt uncomfortable.

'If she fucks like she waitresses, she'd wear out the whole god dam restaurant. I'd only last half an hour.' Dave's talking about Dina who is on duty, while he is busy checking that we have the right TV channels for tonight's Chavez fight and the Chicago Bulls who also have a game. This involves a lot of juggling with his reading glasses as he strains to read the TV Guide, the numbers on the remote and the numbers on the screen.

'You wouldn't last two minutes, Dave.' I reply, but deep in concentration he doesn't hear me.

Dina is young, maybe 19, and quietly self-assured. She's short, but tall enough to wear heels when she wants to and get away with it. Despite long curly black hair, her good looks are Tomboyish.

Dave continues, 'Last night I dreamt I was licking her pussy and she loved it. I was the first person to do it. All these Mexican guys, you know Henry, are all so young and fun and full of come that all they do is stick it in and finish. I woke up in the middle of the night embarrassed, as my little thingy had gone all hard.'

It transpires that Dave has gotten laid with Faviola, the accountant's little cousin, after what is – for him – a very long time without sex which explains his happiness. I pass her on the stairs on my way in. He had been contemplating flying in one of his girlfriends from Costa Rica or Honduras, where he's recently had other restaurant operations. It seems that he's working his way through Central America, getting kicked out of every country on his way back to the States, for not paying taxes. The end goal isn't clear, though. We never discuss that. For now, at least, the circus is in town.

'That's the best chicken dinner I ever had – and you know what? She sucks as well. I just pointed down there and she worked the joint. And you know what?

Goddammit Henny, you know I'm so fucking pissed at that chef Toni. Last night he tried to fuck Faviola knowing god damn well that she's mine. We were just starting to kiss – nice lip kisses – and I'm fucked if he's still not waiting for her in the corridor. She was obviously really paranoid, didn't want to stay, embarrassed I think about doing anything with Toni there.' It occurs to me that Toni was trying to protect Faviola from Dave but I don't say anything.

Toni was head-hunted by Dave in an uncharacteristically shrewd move. Dave simply asked around town 'who makes the best pizza?' then he visited all the contending restaurants and stumbled on Toni's place. But being the best pizza chef wasn't good enough; the chef Dave was after would also be able to build his own traditional Italian pizza oven for himself. In other words, not finding such a chef would mean not having the best pizza in town, and he might as well have given up. But Toni had it in spades, his toothless grin and twenty-something beer gut oozed underworld charm. That he was the accountant's cousin and not obverse to setting Dave up with prostitutes now and then also swung it in his favour.

Dave is back on the Slim-fast shakes, which he hides deliberately on a high shelf that he can't reach without help. The beer delivery man has been so I can fill the fridges, and apparently our licence came through so we can start charging for drinks – given away for free up until now – which is also putting a smile on Dave's face. It's Thursday, so we are guaranteed late-night orchestra income after the musicians have performed across the street in the Teatro Juarez. The players will all come in wearing dress shirts and jackets with bow ties undone in need of beer and pizza.

*****

'I love you man,' Buck is shouting from the other side of the restaurant, demanding that we do a flying head-butt. We collide in the centre of the room.

'I love you too, Buck.'

'Session on.' He produces a small hip flask from his briefcase, takes a swig, then hands it to me. The bitter-sweet taste of Tequila burns my throat but goes some way to removing the pain in my forehead. I get two lime wedges from the kitchen and bite into one, offering Buck the other.

After the shift we head up the street to Rocinantes and sink a few cold ones with the orchestra crowd, but not before Dave has hoisted up the window of his office-cum-bedroom and shouted down to me, 'Hey Henny, don't take it in the mouth!'

Rocinantes is our local, which never closes except on Mondays when it doesn't open at all. Not much to look at from the outside. The walls of the steep staircase leading straight up from the street are daubed in printed hands; a theme which runs throughout the slightly dingy interior. But there's a balcony, and a pool table through some saloon doors. The toilet is a bucket behind a plastic curtain. On occasion they serve pig's-head tacos, but the main specialty is cold beer, plain and simple, and it's the only bar in town that has my Dos Equis oscura, a rare find. The owner, Pompeiio, is our friend and he extends courtesies such as lending me his treasured pool cue, or giving us credit until the next day, plus putting up with our shit which usually runs into the small hours of dawn, and even morning. I think maybe every twenty-one-year-old has a time like this where everything he touches turns to gold. Where he works becomes popular because of him, local bars are full on the back of his goodwill, money is an afterthought, it's all done on charm and of course the ladies fall at his feet. This was my time.

Rocinantes isn't the kind of place where people meet to share a beer or two and dance. It's somewhere to get drunk, or get drunker and I don't think much business was ever done under the fancy walls of cut mirrored-glass and gaudy hand prints. That world, the real world, could be left at the foot of the stairs. And whatever the nature of your troubles, they will not follow you in from the dark alleyway below.

It was turning into an all-nighter.

'Ah yes, Venice: pizza, prosecco and pussy!' Proclaims Buck from the balcony, to anyone who will listen.

Not bad from a guy whose trademark cat-call 'I would crawl on my belly like a reptile through ten miles of broken glass and stompen dog shit just to hear her piss into a tin cup over a pay phone...carrying the quarter in between my teeth,' was heard every time he saw a pretty girl.

We drank beer until Pompeiio's freezer was empty, then switched to Bacardi and Coke until the Bacardi ran out. Then we drank Charranda and Coke. Cigarettes were Marlboro Lights while we could still afford them, then Winston's, and finally Faros which you could afford with your eyes closed but you ran the danger of tearing a lower lip or two if you forgot to lick the rice paper before putting them in your mouth. The conversation was unnecessarily preoccupied with love (hence Venice). Unnecessarily, because we were all too young for that shit.

Whenever she got the chance, Dina would come up behind me and put her hands over my eyes. Then she'd caress my stomach with her long nails. At the end of the party she crouched down and sucked my dick in the street, begging me to take her to bed. I did of course but when I woke up, she was gone. I lay awake trying to work out why we had been playing pool for Buck's face. What did it mean? And who was Dina, anyway?

*****

Dina has been hanging out with two meat-head fucks from West Virginia lately. As a family the West Virginians all have thick necks, physically as well as metaphorically, even the mom. In my heart I know that she's fucking the blonde one; he's a pilot the family have come down to visit in their Winnebago – but my mind won't have it. Still, the pangs of sexual jealousy are clawing at my insides and I imagine she's seeing him which is why she's temporarily invisible around town.

To interrupt my thoughts there is a polite knock at the front door, which is in fact wide open. I call for whoever it is to come in, as I'm not quite done throwing up. My visitor refuses to enter so I walk as far as the open front door and greet him in my boxer shorts.

Fernando, the toothless gang leader, offers me a warm beer and I want to wretch again. 'Ah, no thanks it's a little early for me.'

My new house is at the top of a hill, which like all the other cerros is run by a teenage gang. I made friends with our bandilleros the day I moved in by buying them – Fernando, Sergio, and Burro – a couple of caguamas and a packet of smokes. In return I have received lifelong protection and a nightly escort home. Fernando is the gang's leader. He could be fifteen years old, he might be twenty-eight, it's hard to tell as the booze and the fighting have taken their toll. These guys look harmless enough, I'm more scared of the dogs in our neighbourhood, but they nevertheless go to battle with knives, or chains, or fists, whatever the nature of that evening's rumble is. Yet it still seems very innocent, with no sign of drugs or guns, or even girls. Just combs in back pockets, beers, cigarettes, bandanas and vests or teeshirts tied up to purposefully reveal bulging midriffs.

Fernando explains that he's come to apologise to me as a brother, for the behaviour of some of his banda in the bar the other night when they wanted to attack Buck. He says that the matter is being taken very seriously and will be dealt with internally.

'Maybe I will have that beer...'

*****

By day the intricate network of alleyways and roads was hidden by brightly painted houses so that town from a distance looked like a multicoloured mosaic of emerald green, eggshell blue, pink, yellow and red. Flashes of colour seemingly daubed on the hillside by a carefree hand. At street level there were yellow houses with blue doors, brown houses with white trim and lilac houses with burgundy doors. What made Guanajuato less Hollywood than its neighbour San Miguel, was that this beauty was not so regimented, and you could still find tumble-down stone-built houses and crumbling churches even in the centre of town. By night with the university at its centre, Guanajuato was lit up like a jewellery box. The tunnels themselves were constantly shrouded in mystery and few people explored them properly, either out of fear or simple ignorance that they were even there. El Pípila stood strong over everybody, his oversized right arm seemingly powerful enough to start a whole revolution all by itself. Cervantes had never set foot on Mexican soil I'm sure, yet the guanajuatense people felt the need to celebrate his life and work with statues and even an annual festival. It was just one of the eccentricities that made this town so appealing.

For someone like Buck, the city's architecture and layout made it a good place to disappear; learn a few shortcuts here, and no-one is ever going to find you.

VEINTITRÉS

Criminally hungover the noise of empty gas bottles rang through my ears like a kid playing drums with saucepan lids. It didn't help that the noise was coming straight to my bedroom door as the gas for our water heater was being replaced. This meant that I would have to get up and be civil to the guys and pay them. Luckily I was still drunk enough to accomplish all this and buy cold milk and bananas in the shop, make breakfast and say goodbye to Dina as she was going to work before the second phase of hangover kicked in. After I threw up I went back to bed and tried to ignore the barking dogs so I could grab some more sleep. I would wake up and walk to the Presa at the hottest time of the day. Lazy to cook I bought a packet of tortillas, and threw them into my little ethnic shoulder bag with a banana and a couple of satsumas. I decided that I didn't want to go through town and see anyone I knew, so unfortunately wouldn't be able to buy an ice-cold agua in the jardín. I would buy water and Diet Coke locally and then walk the long way round the periférico to join the path out of town behind the Doberman house where Jenny used to stay. Unbeknownst to me Jenny was already on her way to mine.

I flinched past the various guard dogs and stray dogs who ran at me barking as I left our cerro and started walking past the more affluent houses on the ring road.

These were the people with grass lawns, a true sign of wealth. I wondered, not for the first time, why they didn't also have swimming pools? Maybe they were all indoor pools, or hidden round the back? Inevitably there were basketball courts all over the place and then town just stopped. One or two municipal buildings; water works, electricity headquarters. Prison services. And then nothing until the dams and the mines. I sat under a tree for shade and some water, and waved back at school kids in their bus who were madly gesticulating, leaning out of the windows and shouting, 'Guero, guero!!' A nearby horse was chewing on a plastic bottle.

After a kilometre or two I took a sandy road to the mine and the Presa de le Soledad. This was not my normal route and it was hotter and longer. The usual walk, which included a swim in the stream and shade in the cave above the lake at the end, was out past Jenny's old house. This road was new and purpose-built for the mine vehicles which were big and noisy. I climbed to a view point high above the mine and its busy comings and goings on the one side and the impressively large and deep Presa de la Soledad on the other, and determined not to go back the same way. Sixteen-wheel earth movers with monster tyres were not conducive to hiking with a hangover. I surmised that the older footpath above me would cut across the hill to the flooded village on the way to the abandoned church and mine I normally approached on a different road, eventually leading to the Presa de la Mata. It was hot now and I had all-but finished my water, another motive for linking up with the other path which I knew led to a cool stream. As I crested the hill, something magical happened, the dusty and violent workings of the mine were replaced by softer corn fields of deep green, much easier on the eye.

Farmers dressed all in white reminded me that Mexico was still in touch with its past. I had been walking for several hours when I reached the church and went inside to make my superstitious pilgrimage to the black cross. I took off my bag and climbed the stairs to the loft where, as always, the multicoloured drying corn husks lay undisturbed. From here I could see the old silver mine and made up my mind to explore inside on another trip. I climbed down and looked around inside trying to pray, trying to visualize how many hands and feet had trodden the hard earth floor before me, knelt in supplication before this cross.

The black cross of Tezcatlipoca, whether painted by the Spanish or the Mexicans themselves still represented the same thing. That the Mexican creator was looking over his people. The orange light which fell through the broken window in the roof bathed the floor in a golden hue and I followed the shadow of the cross to a corner of the room where I was drawn to an anomaly in the floor.

I scraped the earth and found a trapdoor revealing steps leading downwards. By my right hand I found a light switch, which to my surprise worked and lit up a long row of bulbs running into the darkness. I followed the stairs down until they led to a tunnel supported by wooden lintels. From here there were two choices as the tunnel ran both left and right. I went right and after two hundred yards found steps rising again to another trap door. I pushed hard and it opened onto what I instantly recognized as the old silver mine. Perhaps the most puzzling aspect to all of this were the electric lights. This meant that somebody else knew about the tunnel. I went back down, closed the trap door and headed left. This tunnel was longer and felt older. I also suspected that it was used less frequently, and as I pushed on it smelled damp, and the walls and floor were more claylike than sandy. I guessed I was under water. Under the flooded village? The second tunnel eventually came up a steep and narrow winding staircase. The steps were made of stone, but slippery and wet with water. The trapdoor above me felt heavy. Was that the weight of water pressing down on it? I pushed hard and the wood collapsed, but I was not drenched by tons of falling water. I was now in an unlit stone vault, and could hear aquatic noises just the other side of the stone wall. It had to be a crypt underneath the flooded church. I retraced my steps, exited Tezcatlipoca's abandoned church and carried on to the stream for a swim in my favourite rock pool. I perched on one giant boulder with my back to another and enjoyed the shade, eating orange segments and tortillas with yellow cheese. I dived into the rock pool again. What did the tunnel mean? Somebody was smuggling silver from the abandoned mine? Or maybe hiding some other contraband there? What was the older tunnel for, between the two churches? An escape route away from the Spanish conquistadors? Somewhere to hide religious artefacts? I was excited and couldn't wait to tell Buck, Aldo, Dina and Jenny all about it.

My second trip to the secret tunnel, and I hadn't told anyone. I had planned to bring Aldo, but hadn't seen him. Dina was on the list but something held me back, and Buck. Well, Buck was busy and hadn't been around. In fact I hadn't seen either of them for what seemed like weeks. What did I think I'd find? Wasn't I scared? I told myself that I'd make an important archaeological discovery and then impress everyone by letting them in on it.

Much as I loved town (Quanax Ranax, Qunax Huato, had become home) this is where my soul really started to sing, as the sierra madre started to open up behind the city and run away towards the horizon. The long way round is a walk of several hours and would take me past the new, operational mine, as well as Presa de la Soledad – complete with sunken village in its centre – before I even got to the foot of the giant rock face which was the climb to the top of my dam, Presa de la Olla, and the entrance to my secret world.

The abandoned mine, the ghost village, the corn-drying-church complete with black cross. Each time I visited and marvelled at the beauty this happy valley, I would see Mexiacn peasants – peons – at work in the fields reaping corn or down by the river washing clothes. Were they even real people? Which villages were they from? What time were they from? I really had the impression that anybody who walked far enough out of town could step through the mirror and experience a better, older Mexico which lay parallel to it the whole time. For me it was an obsidian mirror and I had no problem accepting that I might have my eyes opened there, or my perceptions altered. That each time I visited, in the same field at the same time I saw villagers was a clear sign. The black cross was not a clue, it was the grail.

Inside the tunnel again the electric lights suddenly went off and I wasn't quite sure whether or not to continue. The tunnel was dark, damp, and silent. What lay ahead was almost certainly a pathway to one of the mines but I was suddenly filled with fear. I took deep breaths to steady myself and have a look around with the torch I'd bought with me just in case. The cable connecting the light bulbs did not appear to go further into the gloom, although I couldn't see brilliantly. Was there a turning that I hadn't seen? I didn't think so. I was loathe to turn my back on the unknown blackness but had no choice if I wanted to return to the church. Then I heard something.

I turned off the torch and listened. It wasn't a noise, more like a presence. A very negative presence, something had happened here, something bad. I turned the torch back on but still felt the walls closing in and I ran – hunched over so as not to bang my head – back to where the tunnel was wider and deeper underneath the crypt. I paused again for breath and conquered my fear;

telling myself that it was irrational. Yet I could visualise the tons of rock exerting untold pressure on the tunnel and my fragile body, and was glad to get out into the sunlight again.

The days remained hot, with no respite. All day and night at work I am thinking about the tunnel and the treasure. I haven't told anyone yet, but Buck hasn't been around to confide in. I want to tell Dina and take her there – to impress her – but my sixth sense tells me not to.

The climb out of town didn't take too long, but I ran the gauntlet of dogs in any direction. Some bit me on the leg or the groin, and some didn't. The reward was the peace and quiet offered in the hills and the abandoned silver mines and the dams full of water, so close, and yet so empty of other people. Presa de la Soledad in one direction with the rooftop ruins and church steeple of the village they flooded in order to build it still evident above the water line, and Presa de la Mata – my own personal nirvana – in the other direction which took me past another abandoned village, and a different empty church as I went to sit and write under a tree, or to crawl under a rock and sleep if it started to rain.

The third trip, I woke up hungover as usual, and it was gas delivery day again with empty cylinders being rolled unceremoniously across the cobbles filling my head with unwarranted noise. The blind-in-one-eye gas boss did all the talking while his much taller and lankier sidekick wielded the full canisters at 50kg apiece, and helped the boss to count them on and off the truck. At least it drowned out the dogs barking, and the cocks crowing.

Somewhere nearby church bells had started a chain reaction that was echoed and copied by churches across the valley and down in the town. The new mines were also awake, as indicated by loud dynamiting. So, all in all, a pretty normal Mexican morning for me. Had they no respect for men who'd only crawled home at the first light of dawn?

I made myself throw up and started to feel better. I pulled on a teeshirt and walked out of the garden gate, crossed the alley in bare feet and boxer shorts and bought cold milk. Back in the house I mashed up a banana with a fork and made a milkshake, downing it before the bits of banana sank to the bottom. I lit the gas and made scrambled eggs with black pepper, chilli and fresh coriander. After eating I took a shower outside and thought about heading out into the hills. It was my night off at Chicago's so I could walk freely for nine or ten hours if need be. I hadn't been up to the Bufa for a while but felt it was too touristy. I didn't want to see anyone while my hangover had still not lifted. I decided to climb up from my place, and packed accordingly; a book, a Diet Coke and a cold bottle of water from the shop, a packet of flour tortillas, queso amarillo, and an orange. Up the cobbles past the gas men still busy delivering, past the fruit and veg. market which offered cool shade at this time of the morning and smelled inviting. Even the butcher was spared the flies and the stench of blood at this time of day, which would all kick in in no time at all as the sun rose in the sky. Heading out this way avoided the gang and the crazed guard dogs and it was a peaceful walk until the last houses and hotels had to be negotiated at the edge of the periférico because here there was another belt of feral dogs, mixed up with tethered horses and chickens indicating poorer homesteads. I avoided the dogs, looked down and fantasised about one day owning one of these big houses with a perfectly maintained green lawn, wondering again for the umpteenth time why Guanajuato had so many basketball courts and no swimming pools?

The day's abnormally high temperature did nothing to slow me down and if anything, put extra impetus into my legs as I strode uphill. After all, this was my path. I quickly reached the outskirts of the abandoned village, and paid homage to Tezcatlipoca's black cross in the abandoned church on my way through. The river bed presented its usual giant boulders which I scaled, jumping from one to another of them as white water gushed below. I stripped and leapt into my favourite pool of clear water. I carried on and climbed the black rocks of the dam wall, still at a fair crack, and did not even stop to turn around and admire the view from the top. I walked and walked and climbed again, until finally I rested under my favourite tree, where I could overlook the lake, the abandoned mines and the edge of town somewhere far away in the heat haze. Here it all was, my Happy Valley. The sun sat high in a pale sky, emanating white heat across the undulating plains below me, and onto the red earth that surrounded me.

'Muy buenas tardes, señor. You've chosen a very beautiful spot.' The voice was calm, and I was hardly alarmed as I realised that someone was talking to me from the cave where I sometimes sheltered in rainy season.

'So, it would seem, have you,' I said.

'Sí, cláro. Indeed. Won't you share some pulque with me?'

I couldn't think of anything worse and felt pretty foolish when I asked, 'Is it cold?'

'Si señor, muy fría. Pruébatelo.'

I drank the cold beer, and really for the first time studied my new companion.

'It's my first time to see anyone else up here.' I pointed out.

'Oh, that. Yes. But I've been coming here since long before you were even born.'

'You're from Guanajuato?'

'Más o mènos. Sí. Toma más. Drink more. It is a long time since anybody worshipped the cross of Tezcatlipoca. Now there is something he would like you to do for him. Open your mind and your heart. Who do they tell you I am?'

'Either a messenger from the gods...or,' I hesitated. 'You *are* Tezcatlipoca.'

'Very good,' said Tezcatlipoca. 'Sigue tomando. Keep drinking.'

I took another swig.

'Your friend Buck has something that belongs to me and I need your help to get it back. He guards it well but you must strike before my enemies move to take it. I cannot be seen interfering in this affair. Once your task is completed, you will face a difficult decision. You have already chosen well. You have recognised your Lord.'

'Truly; lord of the near and the nigh.' I laughed.

VEINTICUATRO

I spent the next morning navel-gazing and playing guitar. Dina paid me a surprise visit, and played the perfect artist. When I asked as nonchalantly as possible where she'd been, she simply said she'd had to do something and didn't want to wake me. I let it slide. She had a sketch book under her arm and a box of watercolour paints. When she'd finished painting the view she went to the shops and bought lunch, making a point of showing me that she could eat jalapeños whole.

We slept in the afternoon; she smelled of Teen Spirit roll-on and ptuli oil. Her long black hair fell all over my face. We had sex twice listening to The Rolling Sones' *Black n Blue* on my record player.

It was dark when we woke up but still hot. Or humid I should say, and it looked like we'd missed some rain. We showered together, killed a couple of scorpions with the broom and headed down the hill towards town. With Dina in-tow it was impossible to feel threatened. We waltzed past Fernando and la Banda and below them bought two caguamas. The little bottle store didn't have menthol cigarettes – Dina's preferred smokes – so we left it. I would normally have gone straight down the steps to come out in the old square and cobbled high street near the cathedral but she knew how to cut across higher up the hill to hit the university steps and come down behind the jardín.

The plan was to go for tacos, and get there early enough to beat the rush at our favourite place which was a father and daughter run cart that out-sold everybody else partly through word-of-mouth reputation but also because they made easily the best food. The old man had a big gut and a handsome moustache and was skilled with his cleaver. He could chop meat and onions and cilantro whilst cradling ten tacos all individually wrapped in grey paper between his fat fingers. It was quite a feat. The daughter took the money, popped open the bottled soft drinks and collected plates if you were inclined to temporarily use one. She also doled out salsa onto the finished tacos from her father. We were both excited to eat there again and were also looking forward to a few drinks later on.

I thought I detected a movement in the alley up ahead, then the familiar 'tchee tchee' hiss, which usually pre-empts the call of 'guero' or 'guera.'

'Qué onda, guero?'

It was a menacing challenge, coming from the shadows. Guero was the in-vogue term for gringo and could be simply an adjective for anyone white or non-Mexican, but it was usually used in a derogatory manner.

'Donde está tu amigo? El Viejo.' Where's your friend? The old man. Meaning Buck.

A glint of metal flashed in the orange glow of a nearby street lamp, indicating that the invisible owner of the shout had a blade. My stomach started to knot.

I thought for a second that this might be one of my local banda, sent to watch out for us, but as he stepped into the dim light and I didn't recognise him I guessed he was from a rival gang and that spelled trouble.

'I wanna speek wi' jour fren'. He has a-som-a sing I wan'.'

'So why don't you ask him?'

125

'I ham a hasking heem. First I leave a message wi jou!'

As the man stepped forward waving the knife in my face, I felt a slight nick in my thigh and realised that a second assailant had stabbed me in the leg from behind. Pain would come later. I told Dina to run but she insisted on staying and started to attack the first guy, kicking him in the nuts as he tried to cut her with his knife. My attacker also turned his attention to Dina and I jumped on him as he made to grab her.

'No you don't you fucking bastard!' I managed, and bigger than him my force threw him against the wall of the alley. I kicked him as he fell down, making sure to stamp on the hand that still held the knife which quickly clattered into the pathway-cum-open-drain.

More footsteps ran up behind us and it was Fernando with both Sergio and Burro in tow. As leader of the gang Fernando made sure that Dina and I were safe and unharmed while his henchmen went to chase the two attackers, Sergio with a knuckle duster and Burro with a chain. In no time at all Fernando had secured his prisoners and delighted in his victory. Producing a bottle of tequila he poured some on my wound which hurt like fuck, and insisted that I take his bandana as a tourniquet, and then we all shared a toast. Fernando promptly started tying the two defeated and bloodied prisoners' hands together for a Mexican knife fight. The idea that these guys were now supposed to stab each other to death with their free hands was not something I wanted to watch.

'You wanna stab-a-my friends? Why don't you stab-a-yourselves instead?' Fernando took another swig of tequila and lit a cigarette, looking every inch the teenage Mexican gangster he was. I admired the transformation from slightly overweight drunkard to king of the hill.

Dina and I got as far as Chicago's where Dave gave me first aid and us another drink; vodka and orange this time. Suitably bandaged we went to get tacos as planned. The next day was Sunday but I managed to find the doc at home where he stitched me up and administered two injections; one for the pain and one for the infection. Then I hobbled off in search of Buck. On a Sunday this early he would probably be at home but if I was lucky he might be in town on an errand or escaping his duties. Sure enough I glimpsed his corduroy jacket and briefcase disappearing round a corner just off the jardín and I sped up trying to reach him. The turn he'd taken took me into a neat little plaza that was unfamiliar to me until I recognized the back of the building where Dina had her apartment. A flicker of jealousy tightened in my belly. Buck suddenly appeared clutching a white paper bag.

'Best pastries in town, man! Where else can you get almond croissants?'

I saw a tiny bakery tucked away under one of the iron fire escapes. The sharp sunlight made it difficult to see anything clearly.

'What happened to your leg, man?'

'I got stabbed last night. With Dina. In one of the callejons behind the university.'

'Shit, I'm going to kill those mother fuckers!'

'It's ok, I think my gang already sorted them out. Buck, these guys were looking for you. They said stabbing me was like sending you a message. What's that all about?'

'Fuck it. I really don't know, man. Let's hook up later, I've got to go home and babysit while Carmen goes to church. You ok?'

'Yeah, I'm ok.' I lied.

CUARTA PARTE

VEINTICINCO

McClure was all business as they approached the bullring in Leon. He'd managed to put Harroldson in the rear vehicle, and he drove in the lead – alone – to give himself time to think. The bullfight wasn't such a bad idea. Buck might even be there with the Mexican wife and kid, if he had one. As he parked under the shade of a tree, he was trying to remember the name of an American painter who'd been famous back in his day for becoming the only fully-fledged expat matador. It wouldn't come. He locked the rig with one press of the key fob, and heard its almost inaudible vibration, put his shades on and stood to his full-height. Anyone on the run and watching would *know* that the net was closing around him.

VEINTISÉIS

Buck decided to take Carmen and little Maximiliano to Leon for the weekend. As they entered the town and saw the increased volume of traffic and people he suddenly remembered that one of his students had mentioned the upcoming bullfights.

'Hey babe, why don't we go? I think it would be good fun for little Max. One of my students is taking part.'

'Sure, Buck. You know at this point in my life I'll do just about anything you tell me. Even walking off a rope.'

'You mean jumping off a cliff, baby, but please don't do that!' They both laughed and even little Max clapped his hands in excitement.

VEINTISIETE

My feelings for Buck are complicated. It is not without love that I walk these streets at night-slash-dawn and sleep on benches under the eaves of those I most care for. The climb home is not always identical yet it is the same. I have no control over the walk, or the night. Nor do I have control over who sleeps where or when but the proximity gives me peace. The bench under my lover's window is comfortable enough but it's also far enough from the window to be almost invisible, or should I say, conveniently forgettable. My lover only calls when it suits her. Whether or not that's the definition of a prick tease I'll leave up to you. All I know is that when the spotlight shines on me it is the happiest I have ever been. So my feelings for Buck: friend; mentor; foil; drinking partner. I admit I am infatuated with him and his story and I suspect with a dipsomaniac's intuition that he means more to me, and symbolises more to me, than I do to him. I know in my heart before it happens that he will break me and rent my soul but I allow it.

He wins crib and we share a swig of tequila from Buck's hip flask. A Corona or two later and I'm smoking even though it's still mid-afternoon. The hours until sunset will pass by in a blur of laughter and small talk.

'Do you remember freaking out last night? It really scared me.'

'Sorry man. You know I still love you, right?'

We were playing crib in Chicago's at our favourite window table. Buck had won three games in quick succession and the beers were flowing.

'You really still see the enemy? Like in the movies?'

Buck thought for a second about not answering, about leaving but instead he said, 'In the jungle we were trained to kill anything that moved. That was how we survived. Those are the instincts I still have if I feel threatened. It's automatic.'

'Do you think you could have killed me?'

'An innocent boy like you?' Buck reached for the hip flask. 'Still, it would give you something to write about right?'

'How come you're so good at cribbage?'

'Never fuck with the army, boy. Not when it comes to playing cards.'

'Isn't it down to chance?'

'NOTHING is down to chance. Besides I can read you AND I know what cards you're holding, so it's easy for me. And yeah, I'm good at cribbage too.'

'This guy is disrespecting you, man. We should teach him a lesson.'

'Are you fucking serious? I'm fucking this guy's girlfriend. He has every right to hate me.'

'Mike offered you money to leave town, right? That shit's cold. We should fuck him up.'

'Who told you about that?'

'You did.'

'I don't remember telling anybody that.'

'Maybe you were drunk, but you told me. Right here at this table.'

'That's why I never made it into the secret service. Two glasses of wine and I'm anybody's. That plus I failed the entrance exam twice.'

'I love you, man. Here.' He refilled our tequila glasses, and I sensed it was time for a flying head-butt.

It never occurred to me that Buck had a different motive to remove Mike from the equation. It was always about me in my head.

When his *delirium tremens* weren't in, Buck was my friend. We shared beers and the occasional tequila in the afternoon by the shuttered window overlooking the theatre steps and watched movies on TV, or just talked and played cribbage. These calm afternoons would be interrupted by him demanding that we stand up and go to opposite ends of the room in order to run at each other and collide in a flying head-butt, locking foreheads like rutting deer.

Buck stands 5' 8", maybe 5' 10" with shoulder-length blonde hair and a big handlebar moustache, his hair almost grey but not quite. He wears the regulation corduroy jacket of an English teacher and his leather briefcase is either always attached to his hand or never more than five feet away from him. It is the type that has a rounded leather handle and a strap which folds over the top with a brass clip on it to keep everything in place. And God protect any man brave enough to try and to get near it.

Discovery or capture could have meant jail-time for ignoring the subpoena to court martial (or at the very least dishonourable discharge) for Buck. Perhaps they'd try and make him out to be a hero? You could tell that that wasn't the issue, though. For him there was no dilemma; you don't rat on your mates, simple as that. They could try and make him go back. In fact, let them try. A friend in the police back at home in the States had checked his file and found that the search had reached as far as the border but then stopped. For now at least he felt safe.

VEINTIOCHO

My other best friend in Guanajuato was a 19 year old called Aldo. He'd had a hard upbringing but wore it well, and his infectious smile brightened up any room. He even had a cruel, cynical sense of humour declaring my new flat horible and lejísimo on first inspection. Aldo had known since childhood that he had a secret, but it was something that he couldn't talk about in such a Latin country, the home of machismo. He had a typical matador's physique with strong shoulders, tapering torso, slender waist and shapely, almost feminine legs. That he trained as a bullfighter shocked us far less than his move to Leon to live with his gay lover. If he wasn't in Guanajuato we knew he would be out of town, training. It never crossed our minds that he might be homosexual, but then why should it have? And what did it matter in any case?

Aldo took us out of town in his truck, an agricultural antique with cream-coloured rims, the type with one long bench seat in the front. Aldo drove sitting next to his sister Sandra, then came Jenny. In the back, fenced in by the original wooden slats were me and Dina with Ernesto Jnr., Sandra and Aldo's little brother and Mike, a French horn player from the Guanajuato State orchestra. We poured cheap rum – Charranda – and Coke into white plastic cups with ice and wedges of fresh lime.

As we emerged from Guanajuato's famous tunnels

we were greeted by green rolling hills and a beautiful sunny sky. Ernesto Jnr., only four, should arguably have been in front but he had refused, preferring instead to be with us, the big people, in the back. Ernesto, his older brother and namesake, had been a successful and very famous bull-fighter, killed in the ring just six months before. We all missed him.

Thanks to an introduction from Aldo, I had interviewed him for the University magazine and asked him, 'Matador [always until the day he dies, a bullfighter is addressed this way], is it true that all bullfighters live in communal fear?'

'Yes, both before and after the fight. But we are not afraid of the bull. We are afraid we will fail.'

'But you must have some fear in the arena itself?'

'True, but our pride and even our anger, pushes it away.'

'Pride and anger?' I asked.

'Pride because we are watched by other matadors, as well as our cuadrilla. Anger because sometimes we get mad at the bull if he is a bad bull.'

'And the crowd?'

'They do not matter. Most of them do not understand. All they want is blood. We must satisfy ourselves, not the crowd.'

We overnighted not with Aldo's boyfriend but with the other novilleros – trainee bullfighters – just outside the ring. A couple of small cantinas were already busy ahead of the weekend's fighting. We wandered round eating tacos and tamales. Cock fights and even dog fights were being staged. Owning a dangerous breed dog such as a Rottweiller or a Pit-bull had become more than just a fad in Mexico in the early 1990's and pedigree breeds changed hands for high prices; canine kidnappings and ransoms were not unheard of. I had to cover Ernesto Jnr.'s eyes while two Pit-Bulls tore each other apart.

The bullfight we were going to had none of the glamour that surrounds the big fights in Mexico City. The local training ring in Leon had been built from adobe and wood, as opposed to concrete. There were to be nine different bulls and 16 bull-fighting contenders. I was surprised by the number of different acts, that the programme had such depth at this local level. The day was sweltering and the smart punters paid a little extra to sit in the shade.

Aldo had already explained that supposedly only one of the bulls would actually be killed in the ring – during the finale – but it looked like no such quarter had been given to the horses. Not knowing what to expect I hadn't come with any preconceived ideas. I knew that death was going to be part of the spectacle. I didn't know that I would calmly watch as a horse's guts were spilled onto the ground, his belly cut open by the bull's horns as a picador came in close. I could not have known that I would watch helplessly as one local man was gored and tossed, his limp body carried from the stadium. Nor that the power of the bulls would impress me so much with their mass of pure muscle, as did the bravery of the matadors.

Jenny sat the other side of Ernesto Jnr. to me and kept making eye contact as if to say 'we could have babies like that, you know?' At least that's what I imagined her eyes were saying. Dina's body language left me in no two minds what she wanted but as she was sitting next to Mike and talking to him and Sandra, I did my best to put it out of my mind for now. Both girls seemed pretty turned on by the whole spectacle of the bullfight.

The youngest matador hopefuls, teenagers, pitched themselves against adolescent bulls, tormenting them with sharp turns and seemingly spontaneous twists of the red cape. Aldo had been busy in a performers-only area but we managed to go and see him at lunch in a small corral behind the main ring where the matadors hung out with the vaqueros and picadors that did all the horse, pic, and rope work. Everybody was nervous and you could suddenly sense that these guys really were risking their lives. A nearby stand sold delicious chorizo tortas and cold bottles of non-fizzy apple juice. The sandwiches were greasey and spicy and we all laughed as chilli made our eyes and noses run.

I was surprised to see the same two black SUV's that had been at Casa de las Brujas, parked under a tree. Aldo, with Ernesto Jnr. on his shoulders, took us to see the bulls in their enclosure a little further away from the hustle and bustle of the big ring, and much closer to the cows that kept them more-or-less sedated until they were moved up to a holding pen in the corral prior to the bull-run and the fight.

Aldo was a somewhat reluctant matador. He may have had the right build to become a champion bullfighter, but he didn't have the aptitude, he did it to honour the memory of his famous brother, Ernesto. A prize-winning fighter who had become rightly famous in Mexico and brought home quite a lot of money in his short career had died in the ring, tossed and gored by a bull. He was also a much loved brother and friend who had died at the tender age of 19.

The vaqueros here were drunk and wore broad-rimmed sombreros with the traditional white trousers and open shirts of Mexican peasants everywhere. On seeing Aldo and Ernesto Jnr. they jumped up to welcome their hero and make a fuss over the boy. The pulque they were drinking was quickly dispensed with and we were encouraged to share a bottle of tequila that appeared seemingly from nowhere.

Back in the ring as the sun glared down on us and the afternoon just got hotter we resorted to cold beers to try and cool our throats. The action was also heating up.

Blood had now been spilled; it lay in black pools against the glare of the white sand. Mike, as a slightly fat person was visibly suffering. Aldo himself was busy wrestling a handsome beast of fearsome proportions. This far into the program, the bulls were now getting hurt. Not killed exactly, but ritualistically taunted by the would-be professionals. Two other matadors fought two bulls simultaneously and the crowd raised its noise level accordingly. Trumpets and drums broke out which no doubt confused the enraged animals even further.

The vaqueros who stood guard just outside the ring, all came from the same Hacienda in San Miguel de Allende, another nearby town. This was a holiday for them, and there would be plenty of fun and games later on at the local putería or brothel. It could have been my imagination but I sensed they were being admired by an older white man, dressed in a big straw hat and suit, not far from the gated area. It was too hot for a suit, I remember thinking, and wondered if this was maybe the Professor I had come all this way to see? Dina handed me another beer and Jenny flashed her a jealous look. Life was good.

For the finale they brought on a professional matador, born in Leon but now living in Mexico City. The role that would have been filled by Ernesto Snr. The diminutive star waltzed his way through a cold and calculated execution of a bull that seemed, even to my untrained eye, to be less aggressive than the animal Aldo had battled and dispatched with style, just minutes earlier. It was anticlimactic to say the least. Ernesto Jnr. cried (I think because he was tired and hungry more than anything else) and it was time to go home.

On the way back, having told Aldo that he was my hero, I was about to doze off when Jenny started to make out with me as the sun began to set. There were chickens at our feet as we kissed. Sandra and Ernesto Jnr. (on Sandra's lap) were also in the front with us which left Dina and Mike alone in the back. I thought nothing of it at the time.

Thought nothing of it, that is, until the next day back in Guanajuato when Mike suggested that we meet for something to eat. He chose a semi-salubrious cantina not far from the city centre, but in an area where none of our friends would accidentally find us.

I sat and looked blankly at Mike, while he explained that Dina is his girl, that he knew I'd slept with her and that he is cool with that, but I should stay away from now on.

'Here's a thousand dollars. Take it and leave town.' He said. Mike folded his arms. He put the cash down in between the brightly coloured quesadilla plates.

'Where will I go?' I said to tease him, quietly angry now, but also jealous and confused. I put my hands through my hair.

'I hear fly-fishing on the Panoi River is good. You take a ferry from Helsinki to Murmansk; there's a small airport there with great prostitutes, then helicopter in. Atlantic salmon fishing – there aren't many places left. Russia, Iceland…'

The sarcasm was not lost on me. But I took the money and stayed. Fuck him. Fuck the consequences. I wasn't much of a fighter but I knew how to be a cunt, how to stand up for myself, and how to get what I wanted.

Dina is a painter and does sexy, Mexican mural stuff, he says. This much I already knew. She was doing one in his house, he said. More recognition. She'd needed somewhere to stay; he gave her a roof; she let him fuck her. I was numb. I thought he'd done well for someone with his looks. I unkindly imagined that his pain must be worse than mine.

I had fucked her in her own flat while the new

boyfriend was away. I kept that to myself in the hope that Mike didn't know about her latest lover, the one after me. She had condom sculptures either side of the bed. It wasn't in any way Kosher. Kittens skidded across the floor boards. We showered together. I borrowed her deodorant and we both laughed a lot. I was hopelessly in love. Later she gave me an abstract painting of her vagina, oil on board. It was good.

Dina is the kind of girl that it isn't healthy to chase. The kind you want to chase because it's bad, but if you'd been a little older you might have realised she'd come to you eventually anyway, that chasing her was only weakening your position. The kind of girl who came from Tijuana (or was it Nogales?), who tied her tubes at 17. The kind of girl who tells you a story about riding a motorbike with an older guy when she was just 14, only you're not sure if it's her boyfriend or her father in the story, and you don't want to ask.

VEINTINUEVE

I wasn't really conscious of drinking too much or of being drunk too often. It was one long thirteen-month bender, and nobody had the power to pull me off that train. Dave might say, 'let me see how red your eyes are, Henry' before I started work if he knew I'd been out. Jenny would worry that it wasn't normal for me to throw up every day, but I felt like I was fine, that I was hardened to it. I believed in the beatific glory of being drunk; from an artistic point-of-view. Believed that all great artists must suffer for their art, that altered consciousness revealed truths that weren't otherwise visible. Why else would we venerate divers who had been deeper, or climbers who had gone higher than anyone else before them? It didn't help that my literary heroes were legendary slosh-heads; Jack London, Malcolm Lowry, Jack Kerouac.

I never craved alcohol, or cigarettes, but after three drinks the two went hand in hand. I was young and high on life, I *wanted* to have a good time and found it hard to say 'no,' and harder to say 'stop.' I even enjoyed the hangovers; the sex, the walk downhill past the gang who *were* drunkards, to the jardin to pick up an ice cold fruta de agua – usually a slightly sweetened fresh lime juice. Then I'd wander down to Tortas la Pulga for two lifesaving, and legendary sandwiches and a bottle of Sidral, and grab a bag of caramelised peanuts on the cobbled street outside the hunchback's hotel for the walk back up the hill, after maybe checking my mail at the Correo. Life was good. *No se puede vivir sin amar.* You can't live without love. And I was certainly, very much in love. With Mexico. With life.

My gang, as opposed to Fernando's la banda, numbered anything up to thirty if the Mexico City crew were also in town. These could be students, expats, friends of friends as well as Buck, Dina, Jenny, Mike, Aldo, the orchestra crowd and myself. The Tee apartment lent itself to big parties; it was spacious, out of the way, and had a great view. It wasn't unusual for us to light a fire inside in the middle of the concrete floor, one group could congregate here while another sat by another fire outside in the garden. There were two liquor stores within walking distance and one within driving distance in real emergencies, which was the realm of my nearest-neighbour Victor. Victor was ancient – 36 – and had a fantastic record collection. He lent me his guitar, gave me a bed and even wanted to teach me the violin at one point after a night-long rum-fuelled vigil. He took peyote and while we began to explore the hills and valleys just behind the house, often walking for hours, he would literally run for days, his stand-on-end hair style more madcap than ever.

Our parties were legendary, with people in attendance from as far away as Leon and Mexico City. We'd hit town first, Guanajuato Grill, Quijote's and then Rocinantes to later walk up the hill and carry on all night and all day if necessary. Bodies would variously be sprawled, dancing, or singing and throwing eggs on to the neighbours below. People played guitar, made love, smoked grass. There were writers scribbling notes, artists painting the walls. The whole time, the hills that ringed our town and gave it its name, were watching us with arms outstretched.

Jealousies were forgotten. Dina would be there. One or other of her ex's would come. Mike slept on the sink and broke it one night. And Buck, always in the background, coming and going like a ghost, briefcase in hand. One minute he was in my face, head-butting me, the next minute gone home. The next minute talking to someone in a corner quietly. Parties rarely finished before first light, and sometimes carried on into the next day, and the next night. Then it would be a question of gathering together all the bottles – seemingly thousands of them; Bacardi in all its sizes, from miniature to family three-litre, red wine, whiskey, Charranda, all the beers; Sol, Corona, Dos Equiis, Bohemia, Modelo, mainly caguamas though, which could be taken back for the deposit; Tequila and the ubiquitous Coca-Cola (cheaper than water, and mixes better with rum) – empty cigarette packets, eggshells and any people refusing to go home.

TREINTA

When Sylvia, my sister, came to visit me at Easter, I took
her to Monte Alban in Oaxaca. I'd already seen the ruins in
rainy season when it had seemed as if the palaces and
pyramids climbed out of a jungle dripping with snakes and
red flowers. Now it was a completely different beast, a
fortress carved out of limestone, perched impossibly on
top of a hill. It was hot and dry and windy and as we
climbed to the highest point we shouted into the wind as if
we'd scaled a mountain. It was a way of communicating
with Mom.

All around us the landscape was parched and
barren. Gone were the dark greens and reds. The
remaining grass was yellow and short. The desert sun
began to take control of me and I experienced a vision
which remains as clear to me now as it was then.

In a holy cave near a lake I can see Tezcatlipoca.
Not now, but then, while he was still supreme ruler, before
Cortes had forced Christianity down the throats of his
friends and foes irrespectively. The king appeared half
human with black leathery skin, and the claws of a giant
raptor in place of hands and feet. He was an eagle
swallowing a snake. He turned to me and laughed as if
somehow acknowledging that he was playing games. The
black half-human form returned and he stood outside the
cave in the sun. His face, half painted mask, half skeleton,

drew closer to mine and I felt a sharp blade being forced through my rib cage. Now the mirrors simply show a reflection for us to admire as we strut like peacocks. Inner space, the explosive power of the mind, the ability to create whole worlds, whole universes revealed through the open theatre of the eye. The pressure building until the outside light is forced out and the space darkens, a limitless space that never once stays still never remains the same colour for longer than a fraction of a second, the human engine relentlessly crashing through flashes of purple and blue atmospheres against a backdrop of a million stars, throbbing reds that open up and collapse into themselves only to come back renewed with double the force, then the spinning grid, the dull pain and the possibility the brain's perimeter is here, a clearly defined wall of all the dots and crosses we'll ever see, the black and white cones of thought through the chaotic pattern of electric sparks which kick us into life. Suddenly, the beauty of life's mystery is within reach, to see it, grab it, the human form propelled through life by a mind and a heart that never stop, programmed long before birth to take a thousand decisions every half-second to keep the engine fed, to maintain the blood sugars and salt levels so that breath enters the lungs and life is perpetuated. The quest is that simple. We walk away from the mother, learn to run and run headlong into the arms of death.

Then, the entire great pyramid at Tenochtitlan and the length of the great avenue were bejewelled by an army of obsidian-carrying boy soldiers. Tens of thousands of foot servants, not just here, but also in Chichen Itza, Palenque, Tulum, throughout the empire. The sun's power was not only worshipped but harnessed. I don't mean to grow crops, I mean harnessed as a giant sleight of hand. The human eye only believes what it sees, not what it doesn't see. The blinding lights are me flexing my muscles, to be seen as beatific fire by my enemies for miles and miles. Yet the lord of the smoking mirrors really does possess the power to look beyond the refracting rays and see the future, he can step through the illusion and transcend time as it is understood on Earth. And it is this power that the sacrificial prince is overwhelmed by just as he puts on the mask and bares his rib cage for the plunge of the executioner's blade. So it is a light show to blind the masses, to subjugate and appease them.

Sylvia had by now found us some shade at an outside table by the gift shop café and was mopping my forehead with a wet cloth, which turned out to be my tee-shirt.

'It was the best I could do,' she said, smiling. She said I was to sip water and Coke until I felt better.

TREINTA Y UNO

The rock climb up to the presa was no mean feat, but we were young and fit and even in the heat it was simply a matter of one foot over the other for however many minutes it took to get to the top. Hundreds of feet up and a new watery world opened up its doors.

Henry was familiar with the more recently abandoned mine workings closer to town. The shaft entrance and outbuildings were unguarded and he had walked into the mountain along the old railway tracks as far as a rusted and newly padlocked gate. On the gate was a pretty straightforward message from the mine owners 'Keep Out, Danger!' It looked as if one shift had just come up from the coal face and getting ready for a shower while the next were punching cards and getting ready to go down in the lift. Pneumatic drills and other bits of mining equipment hung on the walls and there were blue overalls and white safety helmets. Henry thought that the whole thing must have been operational until very recently; perhaps the mid-1980's.

From his vantage point looking out over the sierra madre beneath him, Henry felt like a young explorer, the first white man to survey this kingdom for many generations. The outline of Guanajuato's hills, from the back, revealed nothing of the hidden city within their walls. Henry identified his landmarks, the back of the dam, the valley where the mines once were. He gazed at the mountain he assumed to be on top of the old gold mine. In this soft, half-light the shadows allowed him to see through the vegetation to a stronger outline of something that appeared manmade. He could clearly trace the shape of a pyramid. Its peak/summit would never have been visible from below because it was not higher than the summit of the hill but rather built into one edge of the mountain side. Henry excitedly made a mental sketch of what must be the top of the pyramid and its relation to the paths that he already knew. He would climb there tomorrow and investigate. Right now he would do well to be back in town before dark and his stomach was telling him it's time for (taco's?) pizza and beer.

The next day as planned Henry took the day off work and set out early for the mine. This time he took a path that went up and over the shaft entrance to the top of the mountain. It was a beautiful clear day and leaving town a couple of hours earlier meant that the heat was not yet stifling. Henry was tired having done the same long hike the day before, but had taken the shorter, more direct route and was excited about the prospect of discovering a pyramid all on his own. Increasingly he felt that each time he climbed the boulders of the dam wall which wobbled and made deep knocking noises as he jumped up from one to another, he entered a different world, at once older and simpler; in his mind a much better world.

Henry found what he imagined was the top of the pyramid he had seen the day before, but from such close range it was difficult to distinguish from the other rocks and scrub like plants. Tall cactai surrounded it, with wide open pink flowers, and a layer of grass and creepers had formed a carpet of foliage over the years. With only a medium-sized Swiss Army penknife and his hands as tools, Henry started to uncover the outline of a regular and manmade structure. To find these ancient stones in a pile

148

without seeing them from a distance might be to assume that they were simply a pile of rocks but Henry was now convinced that this outcrop, measuring 4ft x 4ft square and rising 4ft from the mountainside was the top of a pyramid which the miners must have inadvertently drilled and dynamited into. The sun was rising above his bare back and Henry wiped sweat from his face with the tee shirt he had taken off, and placed it across his shoulders. He sat back against a tree for shade and thought about how he could get into the mine through the padlocked gates; it would be difficult, dangerous, and illegal.

Henry climbed, slipped, and scrabbled down to the mine entrance. It was in a small open courtyard next to the one remaining outbuilding and once inside it offered mercifully cool shade. Henry walked up to the 'Danger. Keep Out.' gates and started to look around for something that he could use to break the padlock. Beyond the gates were tools of various shapes and sizes including long-bit pneumatic drills and hand axes as well as shovels and picks, all of which would have done the job nicely. On his side of the shaft there was next to nothing. Henry eventually found a metal spike lying covered in sand which he hoped would be long enough and strong enough to twist through the padlock's reinforced steel like a crow bar. Eventually it worked and the padlock snapped off its hasp. Henry went inside.

TREINTA Y DOS

El Truco 7 was a good place to sit and hide in the centre of town. Luckily it was happy hour so I had a little ice bucket of four mini Coronas on the go at the same time, a small bowl of salted popcorn with red salsa and a bowl of fresh cut limes. Yet Rocinantes wouldn't be open for another five hours. The doctor went past in his wheelchair and I followed him into the Chupilote.

I witnessed a drunkard's long crawl to the church, but also saw the black shape of a vulture on the roof, ready to pluck our eyes out...there would be no redemption here if we needed it.

Much later, after Dina has found me in the club, we do the traditional walk to the little café-cum-cigarette shop where two old women and one old man sell us quesadillas and fags without complaint. It's a ritual that helps to sober us up slightly.

'You never used to be like this.' Dina tells me.

'Like what? Don't they sell beer here?'

'Celoso. Jealous. You know they don't sell alcohol. Eat your quesadillas.'

The waitress-and-chef puts the quesadillas down in front of us. They come in twos and we order two more. Another part of the ritual. The waitress isn't old at all, really, probably the middle aged daughter of grandma who sits on the stool by the door giving cigarettes and change.

The old man takes the money on another chair which is also by the door – old green shutters which are closed for the most part of the day. It occurs to me that it is against Dina's character to be here with me and have this conversation. She would normally have fled. Run off with another man. Mike; Buck; the pilot? Shit, she even slept at the restaurant sometimes, for God's sake.

'There's a reason I'm telling you all this. Don't you want to listen?'

In the alleyway behind the cantina and the cathedral there's a human cadaver, stiff as a board, staring up at the sky. I bent down to check if he was still breathing and felt for a pulse at his neck. Blood pooled at the corner of his mouth and ants ran in and out. He was cold and stiff. I can't shake this image while we're talking.

'I met Buck a long time ago, before either of us knew you. Yes, we had an affair – which is none of your business by the way – but now I love *you*. Henry there's something I need to tell you.'

My world was falling apart. I stumbled outside, into the cobbled street. It's ok for me to fuck Dina. I love her and we're the same age. Mike: I get it, he's a famous musician maybe ten years' older, with a good heart. But Buck? He's married with a kid. He's my best friend. I look up to him. Respect him. What he's going through now mentally with the war crimes thing. What he did in the war. But my head-butting friend, my drinking partner, blood brother shagging seventeen year-old girls? I feel sick. I want to curl up with Jenny and pretend none of this happened. In that moment I hate them both – Buck and Dina. The whole Playa del Carmen thing. The shop. Is that drugs? I feel betrayed, shell-shocked. My chest is tight and I can't breathe.

My mom brings me to Mexico. Later I'm back having the time of my life. I meet Buck. I love him. The Professor inspires me, opens my mind. I fall in love with two sexy and beautiful girls. The Professor knew Buck in the 60's, 70's, before Nam? They were lovers? I don't buy it. Maybe the Professor raped him? Am I naïve?

I know where to find booze – even at this time of night – and buy a bottle of mescal. It's time to get fucked. It's time to get Tezcatlipoca's mask back and set the world to rights.

QUINTA PARTE

TREINTA Y TRES – CRUSADERS OF
THE BLACK CROSS

It was the thirteenth day of May, in the year fifteen hundred and twenty-one, according to Clavigero, that the Spanish general, Don Hernando Cortes, with a thousand Spaniards, and two hundred and forty thousand allies, began the siege of the great city of Mexico.

Upon the silver waters of lake Tezcuco floated a fleet, consisting of thirteen brigs, rigged and equipped under the direction of Martin Lopez, and now bearing, as commander of the whole, the Spanish general in person.

Alvarado was posted in Tacuba, with one hundred and seventy Castilians, and twenty-five thousand allies, together with some thirty horses ; and about the like amount of force, under Christoval de Olid, commanded Coyoacan; while Gonzales de Sandoval, with a still greater power, occupied the city of Iztapalapan, upon the south.

Thus the respective parties were stationed at the heads of the causeways which led from the main land, upon the west, the north, and the south, into the mighty metropolis.

The first great master-stroke which Cortes now made, was to demolish the aqueduct, that splendid piece of masonry which led the fresh, bright waters of the distant hill of Chapoltepec through the blue and briny lake, in a solid cemented tunnel, into the city, and filled its thousand reservoirs.

There were wise heads in Tenochtitlan, to whom the cutting

154

off of this aqueduct was more startling than the approach of the thousands upon the land, and the fleet upon the waters. But, to show the Spaniards that they could supply themselves from the main land, by their boats, whole fleets of canoes sallied forth, and returned laden with water and piraguas, filled with fruit and corn, temptingly ploughed their way across the lake, and entered the besieged city.

One day, however, while a fleet of boats were crossing, Cortes suddenly weighed anchor, and with his sails spread, bore down upon them rapidly, with the whole squadron. With a fair wind the brigs sheared the bright waves of the ruffled lake, while the Aztecs, alarmed at this sudden and strange sight, sought safety by flight towards the land, but the paddles were vainly plied, the swift ships swept down upon them, gaining every instant, until suddenly a burst of thunder roared over the Elysian lake, and the groups of canoes were seen scattered and flying to fragments, as the lightning flash came forth, and the black and white wreaths of smoke rolled in vast billows over the water and mounted to the blue skies. Again, peal upon peal broke forth, and shook the walls of the palaces, and reverberated in the encircling chain of mountains which girded the valley of the lakes, and the heavy balls, striking the light craft, shivered them to splinters.

In the tunnel below the church there was no light save the tallow candles they'd brought with them which were fast disappearing. The evening's haul had been worth it and they all stood to be wealthy men if they could only get the loot past their conquering overseers. The plan seemed good enough, to carry the silver at night from the mine to the church and hide it in the crypt with the other valuables hidden away from the soldiers. Jose-Ignacio, his father and four brothers had worked hard all night and were left with only one laden chest to go back and collect.

'You stay,' his father said to Jose-Ignacio, 'and arrange these chests beneath the church. We will return with the last one.' They were gone before Jose-Ignacio could object. In the gloom he listened to his family's footsteps fast disappearing little realizing that they had uttered their last words to each other. From the crypt he didn't even hear the rock fall that killed them or feel the stab of the electric green eyes and feel the tremendous muscular rush as limbs and flesh were torn asunder.

In the chapel, when he was done, he concealed his exit point, quietly lit a lamp and prayed for the treasure's safe-keeping. The only sounds were the deep-throated call of an owl, scanning the church for mice and fruit bats getting ready to roost in the rafters. Jose-Ignacio pondered his own lack of wings and stepped outside to light a small cigar he still had left in his tunic. 'Only angels have wings,' he let himself say out loud, and he looked in vain for the new moon which wasn't up yet. As he blew smoke towards the stars he saw a shooting star and made a wish.

TREINTA Y CUATRO

Ginsberg at the window: 'I'm going over to the square to write poetry in the shade...'

Bill jumped up from the bed where he'd been lying motionless staring at the ceiling for an hour and went into the bathroom. He opened the basin faucet and stared at himself in the mirror with his arms – elbows locked – either side of the sink. Then he burst out laughing and started to shave.

'Sure, Al, go ahead and write poetry in the shade. Write the hell out of it.'

'Say, where did Neal and Jack go?' Ginsberg asked on his way out.

'Dean found a car. They're driving to Tasca. He plain charmed the pants off an expat dame they met in the Zocalo. He offered her $20 to hire her car for a day but she liked him so much she wanted to tag along. She's even bringing a friend for Duluoz.'

'I hope he doesn't fuck it up?'

'Who? You mean Jack?'

'Yeah.'

'Well, you do got a point. It just depends on which way the wind decides to blow.'

'I guess.'

In San Miguel I saw Neal climbing steps up a steep

cobbled alley and watched as he took off his cap, rapped on a bright red door and disappeared inside. The lady who opened looked furtively up and down the callejon before closing the door behind them and also disappearing. Then later they were four (Jack, Neal and two new broads) laughing and drinking at a café in the jardín. The boys were drunk and had started to throw ice cubes at each and every dog that passed by within twenty yards of their table.

The Mexicans nonchalantly turned a blind eye – wasn't this how drunken gringoes always behaved – but the girls were mad and made like they wanted to leave. Dean made light of it.

'Sure, you can leave us, doll.' He pulled his date close (she was already standing) for one last kiss. 'We are but troubadours under the stars and without your angels' gaze who knows what Mexican mischief we might find tonight.'

TREINTAICINCO

Buck didn't tell Carmen and little Max where he was going, but he did tell them to 'lie low.' Carmen took the hint and shuddered, but she was a strong woman and would stand her ground rather than run; a semblance of normality could buy him time if, as she suspected, he was on the run.

'Perhaps Buck has gone to ground,' mused Henry, 'as per his training.' He *knew* Buck was hiding in the hills. He wished that his friend could have fled but knew the ex-soldier well enough to know that what he wanted was a stand-off. In the hills and tunnels of the mines he would have a guerrilla's territorial advantage.

'It's a possibility, Henny,' Dave agreed. He was mixing the first screwdriver of the day. 'Would you like one?' The question was unusual as Dave knew Henry's habits, and knew he didn't drink in the morning. It must have been something in Henry's demeanour.

'Sure, why not?' One drink couldn't hurt, right?

Dave, the obnoxious, overweight restaurateur with terrible Spanish and a penchant for young girls, had also served in Vietnam. He didn't really say much about his feelings, and didn't really care what people thought of him; but he liked Buck. More than that he thought it was disgraceful that the US Army could hunt him down like an animal after years of loyal service to his country. It disgusted him. Why couldn't an ex-marine retire quietly to Mexico, and live undisturbed with his wife and child? Maybe Buck could use a little help? These were thoughts and emotions that he didn't share with Henry, but he silently thanked him for the tip; where to find Buck and where the final battle would take place.

TREINTA Y SEIS

The mouth of the cave would not be booby trapped – simply because it would be expected by both parties – except arbitrarily. It would be rude not to. These minor distractions would serve to draw his pursuers' attention away from his main game plan which would be to seal them in with rock falls on either side. They would not see the trap until they were boxed up inside it. The distance between the cave mouth and the second rock fall was 22 paces, thus minimising the possibility of actually killing the men sent into the cave. It was a delaying tactic tying up both the rescuers and the trapped men for however long it took them to get out, by which time he would be home free.

Buck knew that Henry knew about the tunnel to the church with the black cross. The only other person who knew anything about it was Dina who had led him there (albeit with a different motive) in the first place.

TREINTA Y SIETE

'Give it up, Buck. This is Colonel Tim McClure. It's over. You know we've got you surrounded! Surrender, and we can end this.'

Buck had no intention of answering and entering into a discourse. He also knew they were bluffing; that they were four or six men at most. His plan now was to evade capture and escape with the treasure.

'You may not believe me, but I'm on your side.' Harroldson gave his Colonel a look that said why are you giving the hostage psychological ground? But Tim didn't care. There was no way in hell he wanted to end his career by killing Buck Buchanan. Unfortunately he was fairly confident that his deputy felt differently.

'Colonel, if I may?' He didn't wait for an answer. 'I don't think you should be telling our man that we are on his side. It weakens our position.'

'Aren't we on his side, Harroldson? You're a young man with your career ahead of you, and maybe you think we can kill this man and go home to sleep, but let me tell you something based on years of experience. If we shoot this man dead, having hunted him to ground, it will haunt both of us to the grave. Buck is wanted to testify at trial; yes, that's how I see it. He is not a felon in my eyes; he is a god damned hero. How we got into this fucked up situation in the first place is anybody's guess. You met his wife and son. Does that mean nothing to you?'

Harroldson wondered what the Colonel would do if he knew that the Mexican Guardia Nacional were, at this very moment, on the way in large numbers...

'Sir, you know that I have the utmost respect for your career track record and everything you've taught me to date. But if you haven't the stomach for it, maybe you should allow me to take over bringing Buck in?'

There was a silence, during which time Tim McClure didn't look at his sargeant, his eyes were fixed on the cave mouth where they knew Buck to be hiding. He took down his field glasses and turned to look Harroldson in the eye.

'One more word of that insubordinate bullshit and I'll fire you so fast your feet won't touch the floor. I'll take your badge and your gun and end your career. That, I *could* live with.' After a pause he added, 'We'll need more coffee, if this is going to be a long, drawn out affair.'

Sargeant Harroldson complied, and refilled his superior's cup from their supplies in the truck. But he made sure nobody was looking as he surreptitiously spat into it.

TREINTA Y OCHO

The troops arrived at the old mine entrance in three trucks with an escort of four motorbikes. Dave watched with interest from his mule at the edge of the trees above. He estimated them to be forty strong. He was pretty certain that Buck was not expecting these guys, and equally certain that he wouldn't want a blood bath if he had to take them on. A fly was busy making his life hell, landing in his eyes and entering his nose.

'Come on, buey. It's time me and you joined the party!' he said to his mule.

The best Dave could hope for was to disable the vehicles and then bamboozle the troops with a mixture of firecrackers and Molotov cocktails. The poor donkey was going to be lit up like a Christmas piñata before long.

TREINTA Y NUEVE

Tim McClure had left Harroldson and the other men who were trapped in the cave to follow his hunch and back track to the church in the next valley. The Colonel now understood that the cave shenanigans were not an offensive of any kind, but more of a blind to keep them busy while Buck was making his escape. Colonel McClure also knew nothing of the National Guard called in by Harrison.

CUARENTA

Buck crawled into a position that gave him a better view of the canyon slope and started shooting with deadly accuracy at the approaching soldiers. This was the fire-fight Buck had been afraid of, and he reluctantly hunkered down to shoot Mexican militia. He was now on autopilot and did not have calculated thoughts about what he would or wouldn't do next; for him it was all ingrained through years of training and three tours in the field. He would wait for them to shoot first.

Buck had Harroldson in his sights and prepared to shoot him through the forehead.

'Stop.' It was McClure. 'This madness ends now.'

For Buck it was the signal he'd been waiting for and he used the interruption to head for his escape route.

CUARENTA Y UNO

Buck emerged from the crypt and became instantly aware that all was not normal in the church he knew so well. He carried two heavy kit bags each full with silver. In a smaller rucksack on his back were one or two toys and Tezcatlipoca's mask, wrapped as it had been since he bought it in Saigon, in a Rolling Stones teeshirt. Sympathy for the devil.

The walls, normally an aged off-white-cum-yellow were now covered from floor to ceiling in bloody murals redolent with blacks and reds painted in a style which he recognized because he and Carmen had one in their home; Dina's.

'Hola, Buck.' Dina was up in the corn-drying loft. She looked different and her voice sounded distant and somewhat strained.

The cross which usually leant up against the opposite wall was now suspended from the metalwork of the glassless central dome. Buck was horrified to see the body of his friend Henry, bloodied and crucified, nailed to it. He choked back the tears, and the bitter vomit that rose to his mouth.

'What the fuck?!' He drew his pistol and shot twice at Dina's position then ran for the steps that led up to where she stood.

'I wouldn't, if I were you.' She warned.

'Dina, what have you done?' He used a gentler tone.

'I am not Dina,' she answered, 'I have done only what was necessary. You should hand over the mask or I will be forced to kill you.'

'You know my background, Dina.' He edged ever closer. 'You really think I can just give it to you?'

'Welcome Henry, or Tlautemoc, as you are now called.'

'Thank you, Master.'

'You can see, Tlautemoc, what must be done to protect the mask?'

'Yes, Master.'

Henry could clearly see his own body crucified on the black cross.

'Dina killed me and you brought me back to life?'

'She is not Dina as you know her. She is employed by my enemy to recover the mask. But what they don't know is that I have a secret weapon; you.'

'Yes, master.'

'You will bring me back the mask, and kill Dina.'

From his eyrie above the valley he knew so well Tezcatlipoca sat and admired his handy work. The valley below was now protected. He had spent the whole night painting niches, overhangs and concealed caves in the rocks with the true spirit of his people and religion; black crosses, red dots, dancing nymphs. This was now a sacred valley worthy of becoming his new seat of power. His enemies would do well to keep away. The boy was nearly ready and would not only bring home the mask but then open the door to a brand new recruiting program so that his army could once again reign supreme in the netherworld and on Earth.

Tezcatlipoca's dream came back to him as he surveyed the purple hills of his adoptive sierra madre.

CUARENTA Y DOS

The news that Buck Buchanan had later been found, should have been good news, had it not been for the fact that they had found him dead. His body had floated up to the surface of the lake, alarming a group of Japanese tourists. The Mexican police suspected that the victim had fallen into the water and drowned. Colonel McClure could see the attraction in such a verdict but his own professionalism wouldn't permit him to ignore the facts; and it was clear as day to him – and to Harroldson – that somebody had pushed Buck into the sacrificial pit. Somebody who had known he couldn't swim? Somebody who didn't want him to testify? Somebody who'd wanted to get their hands on his priceless mask?

'Well, you got your treasure hunt, Harroldson.' He said to the young man. 'Only it's a murder hunt as well now! I'm giving it to you because I really don't think I have the patience or the diplomacy to handle the liaison, in what is bound to be a jurisdictional nightmare. Go for it. Go and talk to the Chief of Police, and tell him it's a Federal case now; that Mr. Buchanan, was and still is, our man. I want him to set up a new perimeter and close this area to tourists, and staff alike. If we're lucky we can still find evidence that they overlooked. And we can start with the register. See who signed in to the ruins in the last 48-hours. Check for North American ID numbers, and

Buck's name.'

CUARENTA Y TRES

For all his achievements as a warrior, there was one secret, that few people knew, but I knew. Buck couldn't swim. I turned my back on the lake and walked towards the jeep, having murdered my mentor and friend. Having sacrificed my mentor and friend. The smoking mirrors kept me calm and focused. They (the gods) thanked me for my contribution. I picked up the briefcase and opened it. Inside I found what at first I thought was a skull, but then I saw that it was an ornate and clearly ancient funeral mask. How in the world Buck had obtained it was anybody's guess, but I knew as Tezcatlipoca's servant, that it had come back into the right hands. I placed the mask over my face and felt myself transported to the netherworld between life and death. It was a hinterland of unimaginable heat. I stood at the edge of a rocky outcrop on top of a mountain overlooking an inky plain. The land seemed to flex like rubber in the heat haze and there were no other living creatures save for a raven which hovered on thermals beneath dark clouds ahead of me, and a warrior who stood opposite, dressed in a loin cloth and holding a spear. The warrior's eyes flashed red and two rods of piercing light struck me (now one with Tezcatlipoca) in the chest. I leapt into the air and found that I could fly. The mask was now firmly in place and I grew magnificent wings which further blotted out the sun.

171

I used my large talons to grab out the heart of the warrior and cast him into the depths of the black river. A white horse appeared in the warrior's place and galloped off into the thick trees which grew close to the edge of the red rocks. I knew intuitively that I was eternal youth. I was death itself. I was even the jaguar which chased after the riderless white horse in order to kill it.

SEXTA PARTE

CUARENTA Y CUATRO

'Don't forget your lunch box. Where's your lunch box?'

Laura was busy in the other room taking off her tights and shoes that mummy had just finished dressing her for school in, while Sylvia finished applying light make-up and putting on her pencil skirt and white blouse uniform in the bedroom. Laura sat on the sofa and watched the TV. There was a scratch at the front door and she reached over to open the door for the dog.

'Laura! Put those tights back on right now, we're late. Where's your lunch box? Ok got it.'

Sylvia was in the kitchen now, making sure that Laura had an apple and a yoghurt drink and two slices of cake for her day at pre-school.

'Come on, help me get those sandals back on. You're not going to school without them!'

Sylvia's house was walking distance from the school, but driving distance from the hospital. They got in the car and drove the two blocks to kindergarten.

'Bye Mommy.'

'Bye baby, give me a kiss.'

Dina had hidden her pregnancy well. It was against all the odds, because her tubes had been tied, yet two home tests and one visit to the doctor had confirmed that she was expecting. Henry had become increasingly drunk and she couldn't honestly predict how he would take the news. Instead, she had followed her instincts and withdrawn. For her own safety, and for the safety of her unborn baby. Knowing that Henry was the father (she couldn't entertain the possibility that it was Buck), she had found herself allowing Mike to believe that the baby was his. Mike had a good heart, and would support her financially. It was a potentially dangerous gamble, she knew that, but one she played out of self-preservation. She had told the truth to Dave. He was the only one man in her circle of friends with whom she hadn't slept with, and it had created a bond of friendship. She felt she could trust him, and needed to confide in somebody in case the shit hit the fan and she needed a quick out, and sanctuary, or help.

Sylvia had a life, but she had made sacrifices in her personal life. Her job in the hospital took up a lot of her time and made it difficult to have normal things like a husband or a family. She thought it was a small price to pay. Her brother had done a lot for her when their mom had died. She didn't really remember mom much and life with her brother and step dad is all that she knew.

Besides, having grown up on a base she liked the discipline engendered by work in a military institution. She picked up the tray that contained Henry's morning meds and his mid-day meal, and started towards his private ward.

Walking towards ward 606, in wing 17, had become second nature to her. Henry was still under observation. In the states he could have faced the death penalty for the murder of Buck, but the Mexican court – fearful of Tezcatlipoca's power – had heard his plea for insanity and communicated a life sentence, to life in a secure institution.

Sylvia wouldn't have taken peyote if they'd told her that's what was in the punch. It's like spiking someone's drink with LSD, something no sane person would do.

Henry wouldn't remember being hunted down and arrested, but Sylvia did. It was the terrible end to an already terrible trip. She was worried sick about where he was when Harroldson and McClure turned up in their big black cars, red lights flashing, with the bad news.

What none of them knew at the time was that the investigation would lead them to uncover not only Buck's whereabouts before his death, but also an illicit drug smuggling operation unwittingly fronted by Carmen, his wife. Mike and Dina were brought in, questioned, and locked up. It was a good scalp for the Mexican police. Jenny, her contract with the university finished, had already gone back to England.

The military police and the local police began a search for Henry. He was wanted for murder.

'You won't shoot him will you?' Sylvia asked, shaking.

'No, ma'am. I'm sure that won't be necessary.' McClure had replied.

Sylvia was beside herself. The hero of the hour was Dave Erf, who took her to one side and explained a couple of home truths that helped her to make sense of it all. There was a baby called Laura. Henry was the father but Dina had never told him.

'I can't look after her forever,' he said, handing over the infant.

Quetzalcoatl had underestimated her old adversary and brother. Henry had been sent as Tezcatlipoca's envoy to kill Buck and recover the mask. The cunning old fox had waited for nearly five hundred years. It was a mere drop, in the ocean of time. Henry's shell – his body – was in a secure military hospital in the Mexican sierra madre. His soul was busy helping his lord to rebuild an underworld army that could recruit others and ensure that the empire never again fell into the wrong hands. Quetzalcoatl gloated at how easily she'd been able to exploit Tezcatlipoca's Achilles' heel, his weakness for human female flesh. Her adversary had been so preoccupied with the traps laid for him, that he had seemingly taken his eye off the ball. Yet...

If it was a game that had been played out through many centuries, it was a game that they both enjoyed. Yet the stakes remained high. With the mask back in his possession, Tezcatlipoca would once again control the flow of both mortal and immortal traffic through the smoking mirror portals. As they fought to control the world they had created, he could effectively choke the competition by restricting its movements. Not only that but, should he be allowed to complete the sacrifice of Henry, he could begin recruiting again and amass a new army of loyal servants for the first time in over four hundred years.

Henry liked to read, and he was busy learning about the jaguar when Sylvia, his nurse, came in with some soup for lunch. She fluffed up his cushions and propped him up in bed. "The jaguar, *Panthera onca*, was found in America and Central America and was related to, but bigger than the African and Asian *Panthera pardus*. The panther, or black panther, was a name for any leopard in its black or non-spotted phase."

As she did every day, Sylvia pulled the chair nearer the bed in order to spoon-feed her brother.

'What are you reading?'

He didn't answer and refused to relinquish the book.

'Come on, open up for me, I've got some lovely soup here. I know you're hungry.'

She pressed the book and the hand holding it down onto the bed and got the tray across Henry's legs. She gently administered the plastic cup of pills and started to give the soup, one spoonful at a time. He was smiling quietly, and there was a glint of the old Henry's spark just before he fell asleep. Sylvia kissed his forehead and his eyelids, took away the tray and arranged the cushions differently so that he could lie down. Among Henry's books was his Guanajuato diary, she flicked through it and read at random:

"Arriving in Mexico City for the first time, at night, is entering a new and better world. The expat is born. These bright, volcanic lights, burn away the dreary old past. The fuse is lit. Already, voices are saying, 'why go back?' I successfully negotiate the change in altitude, the Biblical population, the traffic and head towards Hotel Oxford which I've picked in advance as a reasonably central place to stay that I can afford. It's one of the last rational decisions I will make. As early as dawn the next day Mexico with all of its shiny bells and whistles starts to lure me into the lee of her rocky sea cliffs, boldly making love to my senses. There are gunshots in the little plaza outside the hotel and from my balcony I see the feet of a dead body lying prone under a bush, and hear footsteps running away. There is laughter and the sound of beer bottles being dropped and rattling along the ground. Just as the would-be murderer returns and prepares to administer the coup de grace the police arrive, the thieves scatter and the wounded man is helped into an ambulance. Yellow and green birds that look to me like parrots start to peck at flies in the dirt as a woman comes to slake the ground with a hosepipe ahead of the heat. I am thirsty and light a cigarette. In the room's little fridge I find one opened beer which will do until breakfast.

I wrote a ropey poem about an Acapulcan beggar and threw it away. Memories of Acapulco with Mom and Sylvia. Spent a very hot day on the beach but saw at first hand the blight of 'basura' strewn along the coast. Tons and tons of rubbish washed down to the sea by swollen rivers and swept on to the sand by the tide. Dali-esque frames of dismembered dolls, tyres, bones, drowned and swollen rats (presumably unable to escape brimming sewers), dead fish, plastic bottles, glass, shoes, flip-flops, a child's car, drift wood, used needles, broken irons, ovens – you name it – staring up from the sand and bobbing in the (now murky) water. The clean-up operation seems to be vaguely organised with armies of Sou'westered men tackling the onslaught even before the storms ceased (i.e. yesterday), and restaurateurs and volunteers continuing the unenviable task. Even in the space of one day it was clear that the tides were taking stuff out to sea and simultaneously burying it under the sand – very sad.

Decided that I should also find out about the act of crossing oneself on sight of a gringo – this is enough to make someone even as stable as myself a little insecure!!

Bumped into Dina with Jenny which made me feel much happier. Still looking for a house. I rang a number I'd seen on an advert pinned to a door – but for the life of me couldn't understand the reply, even repeated slowly three times – annoying as the woman who answered sounded nice."

CUARENTA Y CINCO

The shack appeared to all intents and purposes to be abandoned, yet it was tidy in a way to suggest that somebody was at least visiting regularly, if not sleeping there. Inside there was nothing really save for a couple of makeshift shelves which utilised rocks, a small wooden stool and a couple of old tins for keeping things dry. I climbed down to the stream and underneath the boughs of a tree nearby found a set of wooden legs which supported a kind of draining board at one end and a wire sieve at the other. I picked up a tin plate from the draining board section and knelt down in the clear running waters of the stream to try my luck. It was a beautiful day, with bright sunlight bouncing off the water and into my eyes. Squinting, I could half-see shadows of fish darting for deeper waters where they would not be seen by an apex predator like me. I started panning – scooping up half a plateful of sand and stones and gently letting it slip back into the water – based on what I remembered from various movies. I continued in a daze until by some magic beyond my control glittering particles began to appear on my plate. I soon had a small pile of 'shiny' sand on the draining board ready to be sieved. I hadn't moved and was now much cooler, completely in shade, by the time one or two nuggets started appearing. Now I had a lot to think about. Could the secret tunnel be an abandoned gold mine? The electric lights already told me that I was not the first person to find the tunnel; but who else was in the know? I could not be sure that I would ever know the truth, yet I had a strong sense of belonging. Guanajuato was my town. These were my mines. Which meant that it was my truth, and that the truth would come to me.

Panning for gold I was a little boy again with the angel of my dead mother on one shoulder and Tezcatlipoca with his talons digging into my flesh on the other. With hindsight I was being pulled inexorably towards the dark side, but it was a) welcome and b) an out-of-body experience which I wouldn't get to witness until much later, when the dust had settled so-to-speak.

As I accumulated my gold dust and little nuggets I was inclined to run and tell Buck, but some other instinct held me back and I found myself hiding my stash in one of the tins back at the shack where I then buried it in the ground. I was on autopilot.

Work at Chicago's continued unchanged. Days were spent walking the hills and panning in the secret stream. Nights were spent drinking and sleeping with either Jenny or Dina. Dina continued to bait the jealous me, disappearing only to be seen with another man. Then she'd pop back into my life as if nothing had happened, sitting at a table with Buck in the restaurant or cooking supper in my flat uninvited.

I wanted to love Jenny but couldn't. The fact that I knew how many men she'd slept with was a stumbling block. But I adored her and we had a lot of fun together. Her body – with soft, giant boobs and round hips – was the perfect antidote to Dina's boyish figure. The other stumbling block was my infatuation with Dina, and the ensuing jealousy. I was blind to pretty much anything that made sense. Guanajuato was my literal and spiritual home. I was a young man and having spent half my life in the USA and half my life in England considered myself fairly rootless. I *wanted* to be grounded in this exotic, expat paradise of sex and alcohol. That it was beautiful and hot with a fascinating cultural history helped a lot. I was determined to stay forever. To die here if need be.

Those that took notice of me labelled me a drunk I'm sure. Friends, especially the Mexican ones thought I was cute and wanted to look after me. Expat acquaintances were divided, some enjoying my company, others jealous that their lives weren't as unabashedly debauched as mine was at that time. Of course I didn't really care; as long as I got my two tortas la pulga and a packet of sugared peanuts during the day, someone to cuddle in the afternoon and a party with rum and Coke at night, I was ok. I could not stop long enough to ask myself, why am I worshipping the Aztec Prince of the Smoking Mirror? Have I really stumbled upon an abandoned gold mine in the hills of the Mexican Sierra Madre?

As I left the light pollution of town behind me, the moonlight bathed the hills in silver and my shadow fell on the path ahead of me as if it was mid-day. I carried nothing except a determination to catch my friends in the act. The jealousy had become all-consuming. If I couldn't have Dina, no one else was going to have her. But I *had* had Dina; it didn't make sense. I was a one-man army. Soldiers from bygone days marched with me; the conquistadores of Cortes, the foot soldiers of Tezcatlipoca, Spanish and Mexican miners heading to the pits to work, and North American treasure seekers searching for gold. We were ten thousand strong, my army and I.

The Xopilotes are always circling, quietly certain that sooner or later somebody somewhere, something will die. They needn't starve for long. As Henry stares blankly out of his hospital window there is a vulture right there, in the tree outside. Far away, maybe, but near enough to come and tear his guts out through his anus when the time comes. There is nothing else left now, only waiting as the matador waits for the gates.

EL FIN

APÉNDICE – EL DIARIO

I had Thursday alone at the Presa and swam naked – gorgeous, absolutely no-one around,

Worked, then went to Grill, Rocinantes' and Victor's house, home at 5 a.m. Rocinantes now has a pool table but the dick-head dealer who's always after a fight was there and we split (Bill, Rob LA, Scott, Henry, Andres, Victor and his girlfriend). Victor lives just above us and as we drank two bottles of Tequila we went through his incredible record collection. Violinist in the orchestra, but at 38 is a complete rock and disco freak with countless photos of the Beatles, Led Zepp, Stones, Hendrix etc. Hundreds of live bootlegs inbetween playing the guitar and catching up on the Monkee's disco greats.

Thought I was going to die on Fri, 12.30 p.m. to 5 p.m. shift, but didn't. Matt, Hugo, Dan, Nigel, Kersti, Camilla and Gavin came from the D.F. at about 8 p.m. After Cubas at the flat we hit the Grill, got even more drunk and then all jumped into cars and taxis to Pequeño Juan's which was free (usually isn't) and very crap. Dancing kind of sobered me up, but I'd had far too much to drink again and Sall (star that she is) kept an eye on me.

Saturday – the posse went up to the Presa while I waited for Dad to ring (received message from Mazza) with Jenny and Selwyn. D and J fine, nice to hear them – ringing about Ant coming out. Evening early took Aldo up to the Presa – met the others on their way back. Cubas with Aldo, playing Gavin's guitar – down to Chicago's where Chavez' fight's finished. Go to the roof of Casa Kloster to smoke grass with Kirt, hits the spot. Can't get in to Quijote's or Grill – wonder why? Six of us – sin Aldo, go to play pool at R's – all of us play brilliantly, incredible – at the Pasadita the four or five beers I had playing pool hit, and I stumble home alone. The others follow later, aiding Matt.

Ani (couple of weeks back) saying to Jenny: 'I really admire you. You enjoy sex and get it when you can. I wish I could be unfaithful like you and not worry about it. Did you sleep with Leo?' – All this and sober! Leo and Jenny have not slept together.

I had a beer in Chicago's and then walked home along the panoramica. Work with Luis and Sally was tense (as Thursdays always are) but we handled the orchestra rush and I got a record N\$42.00 [new pesos], £10!! So we went to Quijote's and got drunk. Felt sorry for Luis who's temporarily split up with his girlfriend – we got on well.

At about 3 a.m. came up the hill to find Rob, Ali, Mike and Victor still at large playing cards, guitar, drinking and smoking. Spent hours playing guitar with Victor, getting more fucked up. We were the last to crash at about 5.30 a.m. – incredible bloke with magic Jimmy Paige hair. He sums up his philosophy by emphasizing the fact that John Lennon's death upset him more than his dad's. He's lent me the guitar again which is a real life-saver – it's a lovely instrument.

Fri 5th – Pretty funky still drunk/hangover day. Got up at 11.30 a.m. for work at 12.00 p.m., went to change money (for the rent) with Carl Cox on my Walkman. The pencil on the desk in the Casa Cambio place had in English in gold letters: Mr. and Mrs. Robert Tipton announce the birth of Gabriel Nathaniel Tipton,

God's gift to our incredible family.

George, a 72 year-old American at least as tall as I am with huge hands, came in explaining that he's on a carbohydrate free diet – wrong restaurant? – we gave him a plain burger with tomatoes. Barely able to move, he chain smoked JPS (presumably no connection!) and put his napkins into a bag so that no-one would have to touch them and catch his cold. He's thinking of moving down for good as he thinks there's a lot of culture for such a small town. He could be right but I tend to avoid 'culture' that's packaged as such.

Friday – Work at 12 – Azuela (landlord) is trying to take the phone, so we find the contract declaring it 'loaned' with the lease. Angelica (one of the Gringo lovers from the Centro) starts work for a few hours, gets on my tits. Go home at 5 and snooze, feet feel strangely better – down the hill where I end up watching Dances with Wolves with Buck and Austen and people. I drink on Buck who's already gone. We go to Rocinantes and play pool. Buck leaves after huge row over moving the 1 and 15 rule – me and Doug (his opponents) divert his anger – aimed at Mike who legitimately moved Buck's ball. Ends with me and Paul playing one of our bandilleros and his partner. We leave just before 5 as bandit-face is cheating and messing around and (himself) 'nulls' the game. Spliff and bed at 6 or so having 'planned' my project.

Work is too busy, Dina running round like a mad thing getting all my tables' needs before me. Me and Dave get tired just watching her. Cella comes in as well and after a huge group of obnoxious kids everything's cool. Wear Dave's trainers and there's a good atmosphere between me, Dina, Cella and Dave.

Buck's drunk again – we watch the second half of The Empire Strikes Back and all of Return of the Jedi which are brilliant – I knock off and start drinking with Buck, again watching the film. We go to Quijote's but Buck leaves after nearly falling asleep. Doug says he must be troubled as he's drunk a lot lately. Talk about never knowing if Buck's capable of turning on friends or not [I remember that Doug liked pussy a lot and is the first if not the only person I know who said out loud that he was a pussy man and not a tits or arse man – strange when I think of the type he usually went for, thin lipped, flat on top...], uncertain edge – incredible force of character, commands respect and fear simultaneously – thankful that we're friends. Meet Darren studying in Guadalajara via Swansea, Rob (Texas) introduces me (points me out) – Darren storms over and shouts 'I hear you're an English cunt!' – Say no more.

Work was dead and Dina (who had also had about five hours' sleep and came hungover) and I spent the shift recovering. Kimble (Dr. Kody's son) was sent out to get D. C. (diet Coke) and V8 (magic) which I'd never tried before. Jenny, Sally and Marilyn were around and Luis came on at 2 and one way or another we had quite a laugh – pizza, bacon burger and fries brought me back to life. Dina, who apparently likes to draw eyes, said mine were beautiful or lovely which cheered me up no end, she totally reminds me of Arturo, even looks like him – she's 19 and from the border, bilingual.

Hasta early hours at Victor's with Rob, Mike, Andres and Paul drinking beer and smoking grass. Incredible music mix, The Beatles with Tony Sheridan, Sex Pistols' My way, ACDC's Who made who...back to black.

Sunday – today – woke with killer headache at 10.30 a.m. me and Paul both cursing Juan Emeterio. Showered and took Anadin after Victor and Andres had brought the

187

guitar back!! – constantly overwhelmed by friendship here, and went into town to have lunch at the landlord's, with his wife and daughter. Drinking Coke and munching on menudo soup, slowly sobered up. Then watched *La mujer de Benjamin* brilliant Mexican film. Walk in the sun up to Pipila and one of Juan's friends pad. Incredible dry, warm wind – we stand chatting on the road opposite The Bufa. I'm still in film-land, in love with the actress who I think was also in 'Chronicle.' Snacks watching The Bulls, take our leave, get my Walkman from Dave who puts his wig and specs again – hilarious, Benny Hill – have an ice cream, up the hill.

Mon 15th – started with a slight adventure as I was stung by a scorpion hiding itself in the kitchen's hand towel. I knew I got off lightly as the pain amounted only to a small injection feeling and there was no drowsiness or swelling. Paul cooked a wicked lentil soup and sardine spaghetti lunch and I wrote to Jamie. Worked from six with Luis – we were pretty busy due to The Blues Brothers and Dave, Tony and I had a laugh drinking vodka and oranges and running round. Went to Quijote's to spend my tips with Marilyn and Rob (LA) and Rob (Texas) and Mike and Dina. Didn't stay long, long chat with Mazza about Sally and Tom, and Rick's affairs.

Tue 16th – Paul potted plants in tins with home-made compost while I did very little except wash-up and sit in the sun. Bought more paint and nails after lunch at La Pulga. Had a nap before work – which was slow. Played pool at Rocinantes for a while with Luis, his friend Alejandro, Rob (Texas), the guy with the nose and Nacho (who was my partner briefly the other night).

Went to work at 2 p.m. – pretty uneventful apart from getting thoroughly wound up by Angelica who started work. Luis came in with the Mariachi band who would play while he gave his girlfriend a ring for their 1st anniversary. Came home exhausted and played crib with Paul and had a spliff.

Thu 18th – Went in at 11 a.m. to meet Dina to put up posters, but she's ill and Dave therefore wanted me at 12 p.m. – rang Ant before work – wicked chat about music and him coming etc. – very excited – Dave spoke to him as he'd never spoken to England before, and told him not to take it in the mouth. Posted Jimbo's and Emma's letters and got letters from Mum and Emma. Wrote to Mum (Jenny posted it) and Emma again with photo of me and John from Rob (I posted it later). Steady day, new girl works well and less annoying than Angelica who pissed me off again – just her whole manner.

Dave's really been on form lately – hilarious about not getting any pussy, with great anecdotes about his old night-club; (You know Henry I just like to Fuck ....just go home to the wife...).

Fri. 19th – Work 12 - 5 with Luis and Felipa. Jenny and Marilyn persuaded me not to have my ear pierced by Dina. Not surprised it was Jenn, said she'd respect a personal decision more – miaou. Stripped and painted our door-slash-green table – Paul did second coat. Bought beers and played crib.

Sat. 20th – Bought empty crates and peanuts with the shell on. Lunch with Jenny, Sally and Marilyn (who's been told she needs a second root canal), Tom and Jenn's parents. Wicked meal with chicken pie and salad, outside. Rang Emma (v. nervous) and spoke to her dad – she rang back after work, very emotional after such a long time without speaking, felt helpless as she cried, love her so much. Feels so good to be in touch again, other than by post.

Chilli-lentil soup and soya spaghetti; crib; bed. Couldn't sleep, started to read 'No one writes to the Colonel.'

Mon 22nd – Finished Marquez and went into town. Did an 'Isseg' shop for work. Got pissed off at work with gringos insisting on talking to me in shitty Spanish even after Dave has explained I'm from Oxford, England – as if to say 'can't you see you're killing him?' Sonja and the accountant's cousin, like Felipa and Angelica, are so far from my wavelength it's not true. I felt guilty about finding them a pain, telling myself that it's because I'm not fluent in Spanish and they don't speak English but I can safely say that they are just stupid, 'muy serias' and boring. I have heaps of Mexican friends who I only speak Spanish to and I know they get Toni's back up as well.

Luis didn't turn up today, leaving Dina to run around on her own until 5 p.m. or so. Apparently he bought a bulk load of tortillas and has to sell them all by a certain date or they'll break his legs or something – so I guess he was selling tortillas!!

Dave tells me that he finally had sex last night but no-one's sure who with yet. I think maybe once wasn't enough as his mood change wasn't as marked as I'd hoped it might be after the big event. This after all is the same man who was ready to pay any woman he fucked in Costa Rica or Honduras to fly over here, or any willing whore in Irapuato – to relieve his burden. (Lots of thankyou's and compliments on the party.)

Tue 23rd – Good chat with Sonja at work about marriage and stuff. She's 19 with a two-year-old daughter (earning what I get) and her sister at 20/21 has four kids. Barely slept – started a story.

Wed 24th – [Just wandered around, tried to write at Chicago's, couldn't – sat with Doug, good talk.] Really down – work petered out after Dave got the vodka and fresh orange out. Got wankered on Rob and Leo (who walked me home after Rocinantes; Quijote's). Woke up fully-clothed (including boots).

Played guitar until 2.30 a.m. Paul came in at 4 a.m. to get me to help carry a mattress he'd found, up the hill. Got it in only to find bed-bugs infestation.

At 4.30 p.m. Dave gave orders to be locked in his office and spent half an hour screwing some poor 15/17 year-old Mexican girl for $50, 000 (old pesos) – obvious to the whole restaurant what's happening.

Left work to buy a guitar string feeling pretty sick still, as far away as possible, with Emma and Ali who were going out for a drink together.

Last night i.e. Thursday after work, Faviola, the accountant's little cousin who first fucked Dave who works as the cashier, asked Toni not to leave her alone with Dave, so Toni waited and walked her home.

I told Dave what I'd heard – that she hadn't wanted to stay – and he calmed down, saying that she'd said she'd stay tonight anyway.

By the time I go to Rocinantes looking for Paul and meet Rob (LA), Mike (French horn) and Antonio I'm confused and shaky, hyped up, smoking heavily and gulping my beer – so much love in one day and I can't be with the people closest to me.

Me and Mike team up on the pool table and don't

lose for at least two hours, wiping out everybody with some really class play. I calm down and vent my frustration on the table. Great night, beat loads of the regular dickheads earning major respect. Came home and got stoned with Paul, drinking Bacardi, playing cards and guitar. Mike left and Paul and I stayed up until 8 a.m.

Went to the rest. expecting Ant to call and stayed until the end getting drunk on vodka and orange whilst talking to Buck and watching the Academy awards. Good chats with Buck; music, books, accents, world class structures. We went to Rocinantes – but only after I'd extracted his word not to take offence or get upset by any of the assholes up there. Luis stays for a game and then leaves. Me and Buck play a guy I beat with Mike the other night and his friend. Everyone's drunk but we just get on with it until Buck offers them a money game and the guy from the other night (a real wanker) wants to play for Buck's face!? – WOHHHH – I play mediator and Buck uses all his will-power not to beat the shit out of him. We get the owner (our mate) to chastise shit-face and he lets me and Buck leave before the others. Buck's fuming and I can only say 'Thanks' as he explains 'You know I only did that because I gave you my word, Henry.'

Stefanie, Patricia, and Doreen are in Bar Luna where we have a couple while Buck, shaking, explains that sometimes he just flips and anything moving in front of him is an enemy and the pressure has to be released. The anger stemming from Nam jungle combat, I guess. Had a long chat about Into the Heart, how maybe in the end he didn't have the balls to just fuck everything and go native. Bed at four or so.

It was a party on the roof in a part of town somewhere near Rick's place. Carmen would come up behind me and put her hands over my eyes then she'd start scratching my stomach with her long nails. At the end of the party she crouched down and sucked my dick in the middle of the street, begging me to go home with her. Ali was waiting in the car on the main road. I said 'no, thanks,' but was still later accused of sleeping with her by her crazy husband – one of the orchestra drunks – who had apparently raised a posse to come and get me one night after his return from holiday. I later learned by proxy (from Sall).

Having skived college to catch up on sleep I'm sitting in the sun of our courtyard listening to Pablo's flamenco guitar record trying to work out what happened in the last week. I think Sunday night was a quiet coffee with Rob and Aldo in El Truco then a quick visit to the Gallo to hear Lauren sing – which was very good. I've spent time with Aldo every day, speaking mainly Spanish – he's 19 and has had a pretty tough life I think, fending for himself – we're developing a firm friendship. I'm getting on really well with Jenny as well – we had breakfast together yesterday and the day before between her classes. Two nights ago Sall and Marilyn came round to look at Bel Air with Jenny and Lauren – we ended up all eating pasta at Jenny's and after two vodka bottles' worth of Tom Collins's we went to the Guanajuato Grill and had a great dance. The two days of college I've had have been ok but a bit slow. Drew is in our class as is Melissa and five of her six or seven siblings as well as Diana, their mum. Apparently they went through a Mormon period in Utah, hence all the kids. [Now Seventh Day Adventists.] Yesterday Drew asked me out of the blue 'Do y'all have negroes in England? You know, black folks?' I just said yes, too tired to take issue with his political incorrectness.

On Thursday night, having eaten with Jenny and Rob and Leslie in the Taco Inn we met up with Aldo, Melissa and Drew and went up to John, Doug and Ryan's for a party. There were loads of people, mainly Mexican –

I had a good chat with Rosa Marta about acting. The Mariachi band finished me off with ample tequila as one of them explained the tuning of his twelve-string banjo-type mini-guitar. There was a fire on the roof and everyone sang. It was great.

Dehydrated and unable to wake up for college at 07.30 a.m. I slept in until around 2.30 p.m. when Aldo came round in his car to remind me that we were going to eat in the sierra (Santa Rosa) – I dressed quickly and ignored his advice to bring a jacket. Having collected and dropped off Aldo's nephew and niece we waited at his shop for Melissa, Sandra and Selena – at this point a Diet Coke saved my life and I was able to function at a more normal pace without feeling sick. Sandra and Aldo took me with them half way through the party last night to get tacos – I didn't eat – to chat in Spanish – Aldo's great like this 'come on Henry …' Selena drove and we picked up Dave and Austen. Climbing out of Guanajuato in a full car listening to the stereo, found us in the middle of deeply forested mountains. Planed-off clouds stretching far away to the furthest peaks, occasionally lit by sharp sunlight – really gorgeous. After about an hour we had a fantastic meal with sweet coffee and headed down into the forest for a walk amongst the icy streams, mushrooms, and bright red mud. As the rain came and we were split up in the dying light shouting to each other, Picnic at Hanging Rock sprang to mind. We returned cold and happy. I came back and showered and met Rob with John and Ryan (on the pull) in the jardin. Rob and I went to find Lauren singing to Michi's cutting electric organ with Jenny, Sall, Melissa and Marilyn. Me still rough, quiet and lonely. Walking back with Rob we had a gorgeous supper at El Figon of bean soup, asada, tortillas and atole (hot corn with honey and cinnamon drink) for about £1.00. The wind still cold.

Oaxaca at Easter, was hot like hell. The ruins, Chichen Itza, were dry and dusty, not like the humid and verdant jungle I'd seen only weeks before. Sam, my brother and I sweated and swooned our way up and down the pyramids. At the beach, we sweltered in hammocks on Puerto Angel, catching giant lizards, eating fresh fruit, and cracking coconuts with machetes. There was a steady flow of alcohol from beers (Corona, San Miguel, Dos Equiis Oscura), rum and coke, charranda and coke, to tequila with or without Squirt, and always with fresh lime. The hills around Guanajuato turned into desert plains, and we walked and climbed and scorched ourselves, scouring the landscape like vultures for any rocks that might offer shade and respite. We cooled ourselves in cattle troughs. We bumped into Victor, the violinist, running for his second or third day on peyote, wishing that he could fly. He disappeared over the horizon. Nights blurred into days, either parties at the flat, all-nighters at Rocinantes, house parties, night clubs – peppered with pizzas at the restaurant. But this is background. Even the story of Sam disappearing for three whole days to be found whiskey-drunk on the railway tracks where the real-life hero of On the Road, Neal Cassady had died just outside San Miguel – is window dressing. It was the Presa de la Mata and the walk out of town. The abandoned silver mine, and the secret church. That's what we learned.

BIBLIOGRAFÍA

Going Down, David Markson, Holt Rinehart Winston, 1970

Year of the Jaguar, James Maw, Sceptre, 1996

Under the Volcano, Malcolm Lowry, Reynal & Hitchcock, 1947

Malmiztic the Toltec; and the Cavaliers of the Cross, W. W. Fosdick, 1851

History of Mexico vol. I, Clavigero, 1787

Lawrence, Greene & Lowry: The Fictional Landscape of Mexico, Douglas Veitch, Wilfrid Laurier University Press, 1978

Unknown Mexico, Vol. I, C. Lumholtz, New York, 1902

Bullfighting in Mexico: The conquest of fear, Latino style, Shep Lenchek, 1997

The Man in the doorway, Michael Ryerson

SOBRE EL AUTOR

Henry Green was born in Oxford in 1972. He studied Latin American Studies at the University of Portsmouth 1991-1995 and lived in Guanajuato for 13 months in 1992-1993 where he learned to speak fluent Spanish. Whilst researching his thesis on expat Mexican literature Henry corresponded with David Markson and Allen Ginsberg about the mythical Mexico experienced by foreign writers versus the real Mexico and the fine line that separates the two.